Mordec Raids England

THE THRILLING ADVENTURES OF MORDEC THE VIKING

Mordec Raids England
Mordec's Quest
Mordec and the Hidden Hand
Mordec and the Lost Boys
Mordec the Conqueror

THE THRILLING ADVENTURES OF
MORDEC THE VIKING

BOOK 1

MORDEC RAIDS ENGLAND

JILLIAN BECKER

This is a work of fiction. Names, characters, organizations, places, events, and incidents are either products of the author's imagination or are used fictitiously.

Copyright © 2018 by Jillian Becker
All rights reserved

No part of this book may be reproduced, or stored in a retrieval system, or transmitted in any form or by any means, electronic, mechanical, photocopying, recording, or otherwise, without express written permission of the author.

Typesetting and Cover Design by
FormattingExperts.com

Published by Gothenburg Books
ISBN 978-1-7327275-0-2

contents

Mordec Raids England

To my grandchildren:

Matthew & Aaron Slipper
Jessica & Elizabeth Dilworth
Sam & Charlotte Westrop

the skald

Mordec the Viking's amazing adventures began when he was fourteen.

His father Hauk had travelled far when he was young, and in a land to the south had met Estrid daughter of Adam and brought her back to the Northlands as his bride. She had skills beyond those of the other women who lived on the same jut of the jagged shore round a shipyard and large harbour named Trygghaven, to which Vikings all over the Northlands sent their goods—chiefly furs—to be traded abroad. She was an excellent cook, and could read and write and reckon. She brought a few books with her, and vessels made of glass and silver as well as the customary bridal dowry of coins, linens and brooches.

When her son Mordec was five years old she began teaching him her skills. When he was ten he learnt from his father how to ferment the golden mead from honey, and bright cider from crushed apples. Hauk made his living as a mead maker, and had built the mead hall where the men came to drink and listen to stories of heroes. He also sold honey, mead, apples and cider in the market, and to the small traders who carted their wares up and down the coast.

One morning in the spring of his fifteenth year, Mordec was in the orchard tending the beehives with his father when he saw the cart of Hrut the Trader come swaying and creaking over the dune-lumps of the heath, drawn by a bullock the colour of sand. It drew up at the gate. Hrut's daughter Thorgerd the Daft was in it, and an old man.

'They have the Skald with them,' Hauk said. Sigvald the Skald, blind poet and story-teller, was also a seer, a foreteller of destinies.

Hrut climbed down, put the reins in Mordec's hands to hitch over the gatepost, and went with Hauk to give a poor opinion of his honey and mead and gasp at the prices he dared to ask.

The Skald stood up in the cart. He was tall and flat, a little stooped. The white robe hanging from his frail shoulders to his shoes was belted with bronze medallions linked with loops of gold. White hair framed his long, fine-boned face and fell in tangled locks over his shoulders, and a sparse beard twisted down to his chest. His eyes, under white and bristly brows, had no irises or pupils. They looked as if they were made of pale blue glass.

He stretched out skeletal arms. Mordec reached for his wrists to help him down, but the old man had a different purpose. With a sudden movement and surprising force he wrenched his arms free and fastened his hands onto either side of Mordec's head, gripping it as they might a precious vessel.

'Tell me, girl, how he looks,' the Skald demanded. His voice was not an old man's quaver, but clear and resonant.

The girl crawled across the cart, leant over the side, and stretching her neck to bring her face close to Mordec's, she burbled in a sing-song tone: 'He has glasses joined together over his nose and hooked behind his ears with silver but he's handsome and his hair is gold and hay and honey and mead and it falls over his brow and his skin is bright and his eyes are blue as the face of the sky on the iceberg's side.' Then she reached out and stroked his hair with a small soft hand.

'In what is he clad?' the Skald asked, leaving go of Mordec's head and bringing his tapering fingers together.

'He wears a blue tunic and blue leathern shoes.'

'What colour blue the tunic?'

'The blue of the sea in a storm.'

'Dark?'

'Dark.'

The blank eyes of the Skald seemed to search Mordec's face. 'What do they call you, boy?'

'Mordec son of Hauk.'

'Mordec, you have far to go, much to do and much to learn, and many shall hear of you,' the Skald said.

The girl clapped her hands and laughed with such delight that she made Mordec laugh too. She jumped down from the cart and went laughing and singing into the orchard.

When Hrut drove away his cart was full of sacks and pots and jugs, of apples, honey, mead and cider. The Skald sat beside him on the driver's bench, but there was no place now for Thorgerd, so she sat astride the bullock. She'd draped its neck with a garland of grasses, purple mothers-tears and stolen apple-blossom, and had woven the same flowers into her own butter-coloured braids. Mordec stood at the gate and watched them go. His mother, Estrid, came and stood beside him.

'The Skald is a kinsman of Hrut's,' she said, 'and also of Gudrun, wife of Knefrod the Hunter. That's where they'll be taking him now. Gudrun says that Thorgerd had a spell put on her when she was a baby.'

'Who wove the spell?'

'The Troll who lives under the mountain. So they say. But I think she was born like that.'

'She always seems happy,' Mordec said.

'I think she is.'

Mordec told her what the Skald had said to him. 'It sounded like a prophecy,' he said.

Estrid shook her head. 'They say that as his sight faded his second-sight grew until he could see into the future. But don't you believe it. You'd be asking for disappointment.'

'He asked about the colour of my tunic.'

'Did he? Then I know why he said what he did. In the sagas, you see, the heroes wear dark blue.'

'That's the only reason why he said it?'

'He likes to sound mysterious but he's not truthful. Everyone knows it. They forgive him because he's a skald.'

'But he is blind, with eyes like that?'

'Yes, but not with age. He's nowhere near as old as he pretends to be, so Gudrun told me.'

How old does he say he is?'
'A hundred and one.'
'And how old really?'
'Twenty-eight?' Estrid joked.
Mordec couldn't help laughing, but he also couldn't help believing that he was marked out for some special and splendid fate, like Alexander the Conqueror.

half a ship

The ships of the Vikings were the best in the world since ever the world began.

On the same bright morning when Sigvald the Skald prophesied greatness for Mordec, Olaf son of Olaf the Shipbuilder was watching his father planing oak for a new longship. The pale strips rose, curled and fell until the plank was as smooth and glossy as silk. Olaf, now thirteen years old, was being taught his father's craft, but his heart wasn't in it, as the Shipbuilder knew and regretted. But Big Olaf didn't protest or complain because what his son did want to be was a pirate, and what in the world could make a father more proud than that?

'Dad, when will you let me come on a voyage with you?' young Olaf asked.

'When you're grown up.'

'When will that be?'

'When you don't have to ask.'

'Let me sail with you this year?'

'You'd take up space in the ship and be no use to us.'

'I'd take up only half as much as a man.'

'If you build your own ship you can come with me.'

'A whole ship?'

'Maybe not a whole ship when you're only half a man. Half a ship would do.'

Olaf took his father's joking words as a promise that if he could build 'half a ship' he could raid England in the summer. And the gods seemed to be on his side when just a few days later they sent him a half-size ship, ready built, and as fine as every Viking ship must be.

Yet for their own unfathomable reasons the gods let Mordec son of Hauk find it, not Olaf himself. And Mordec was the boy least likely to become a pirate, in Olaf's opinion. Not only did he wear glasses, which a pirate would never do, but he could read and write, and was forever laughing at things nobody else found funny. And he liked to go off to the woods on his own. Of course every boy would *sometimes* go alone to lay traps for birds and small animals in the nearby woods which were safe enough since the hunters had frightened off the wolves. But Mordec ventured further than the rest. And because he risked going where none of the others would, he found the ship.

It was on a piece of land known as Haraldsholm which had lain for as long as Mordec could remember beyond a wide, deep river. Something suddenly made the river dwindle to a stream, easy to cross. On the other side of it Mordec found a ruined village and a dusty shipbuilder's shed covered with creepers. Peering through he saw sunlight shafting through holes in the roof, lighting up swarms of dust-motes in the air and patches of weeds in the cracked floor. He put his glasses in his pocket and tore his way in, twigs and thorns clawing his face. Inside, the glare of the sun-shafts made everything else seem darker. Brushing leaves, cobwebs and small spiders from his hair and clothes he waited for his eyes to adjust to the strange dusty light. Still everything was slightly blurred until he put his glasses back on. Then he could see that on one side of the big space was a workbench, and on the other pairs of cradles holding unstripped logs. The middle of the floor was taken up by a row of cradles holding some bulky object, and as he stood staring the sun struck through a roof-hole straight on to it. It was a ship about half the size of most of the longships built in Olaf's yard.

If Mordec could have launched the ship and sailed it home alone, he would have done. Then no one could say it was not his. But he needed help.

In the evening when the sun was bleeding slowly into the sea, he went to the cave of boulders on the shore where boys often gathered. Four were there when Mordec came to tell about the ship. Two of them were wrestling on a patch of sand, Gus and Eric, both nearly fifteen years old. Gus was the taller and heavier, but Eric more lithe, harder to hold on to. Watching them was Olaf, and Eric's younger brother Bjorn. Although Bjorn was not much shorter or thinner than Olaf or others of his age, Eric pretended he was and called him Titch, so the others did too.

Mordec sat and watched Gus floor Eric for the third time. Eric stayed on his back. 'Give up?' Gus asked. Eric had no breath to answer so he nodded. Gus turned to Mordec. 'You also want to be beaten hollow, Mordec?'

Mordec shook his head.

'Scared?'

'Sure,' Mordec said. But they all knew he wasn't. He was almost as big as Gus and almost as strong. He just didn't need to *prove* he was strong and brave as often as Gus did. 'I came to tell you that I found a ship.'

'What did you say?' Olaf asked, unable to believe his ears.

'A ship. Not as big as our longships but big enough to sail in. I found it.'

'I don't believe you.'

'Then come with me tomorrow and see for yourself.'

* * *

Gus, Eric, Titch and Olaf followed Mordec to Haraldsholm.

'Now d'you believe me?'

It was blanketed with dust, but marvellous. The boys touched it, stroked it, knocked on it.

'Odds-bods!' Olaf exclaimed, over and over again. It really was about half the size of his father's longships, as if it had been made to his order by a magician's hand. And it was almost complete, even the benches in place. 'See the kerling,' he said, showing off his knowledge by naming the heavy block of oak in the middle with its grooves and devices for holding the mast. Only the mast itself was missing.

How long had it been here, they wondered, and why had it been abandoned?

'It couldn't actually belong to anyone, could it?' Titch asked Gus.

'Thor sent it to us!' Olaf declared.

'Maybe it belongs to a sorcerer and if we take it we'll be cursed,' Eric suggested in a tone of awe. 'Maybe we should leave it where it is and go away.'

'Are you afraid to take it?' Olaf said.

Mordec said, 'What sorcerer? What curse? There's nobody here. The whole place is deserted. We're not robbing anybody.'

'Finding's keeping if it doesn't belong to anybody.' Gus said.

'If this one,' Mordec said, 'is under a spell it must be one that keeps it safe. Look at it—not a hole anywhere, nothing broken. It's perfect except for the dust.'

'That's right,' Titch said. 'Let's get it down to the sea and row it home.'

'Won't my dad be surprised!' Olaf said.

Gus said, 'We can start cleaning it today and clearing a way to the sea, but we won't be able to lift it and carry it down. Not just five of us.'

'We need more men,' Eric agreed.

Next evening when the tide was out and the sun descending in a clear sky, Gus brought Gunnar son of Gunnar the Sailmaker, and Mordec brought Horsa son of Harvald the Armourer, to the cave. Gunnar was a quiet boy who liked being part of a team and didn't mind taking orders if he thought they made sense. Horsa was sturdy and strong and could handle weapons as well as most full-grown men or even better. Olaf thought he'd be a fine comrade-in-arms in the battles he was looking forward to.

Gus and Mordec didn't tell the new recruits why they were invited to the meeting place, but whetted their curiosity by saying there was 'a special reason'.

'We'll let you into a secret,' Gus told them. 'But first you must promise to keep it, whatever it may be.'

They gave their word and Mordec told them about the ship. 'So will you help us?' he finished.

'Try stopping me,' Gunnar said.

'Or me,' said Horsa.

The seven cleared a path from the shed to the shore, and cleaned the ship. Finding that some of its iron rivets, though rusty, had come loose from the plates into which they were driven through the wood, Gus and Mordec tightened them. All worked at shaping rough oars out of planks and logs.

* * *

It wasn't long before three other boys found out their secret, simply by following them. They erupted one evening into the shed while the seven were at work on the ship and the oars.

'What're you doing?' one of them asked, strolling about the cradled ship.

'None of your business. How d'you get here?'

'That would be telling.'

'Well, now you're here you'll have to give your word that you'll keep our secret.' Gus said, 'and then help us.'

'And if we don't?'

'If you don't,' Gus said, 'I'll kill you.'

'Aargh! You don't scare me.'

But they all gave their word.

Two of them, the sons of fishermen, were both named Hengist. As one was chubby and the other wasn't, Eric dubbed them 'Big' and 'Little'. Little Hengist was soon to prove himself useful. He had a knack for making and fixing things.

The third, the one who'd argued with Gus, was Kol son of Knefrod the Hunter. He'd been taught the arts of trailing and tracking, and these skills had got them here.

Kol was a sallow-skinned, lanky boy with droopy eyes. He shaved the sides of his head and tied up what was left of his hair in a knot on his crown, as his father did. He always spoke as if he had a slightly blocked nose, and when he was not speaking kept his mouth hanging open.

'What's *he* doing here?' he said nasally, pointing both his forefingers at Mordec.

'Shut up, Kol!' Gus said. 'When you've heard what we have to say you'll know why he's here, and then if you don't want to be where he is, *you* can leave. Got it?'

Mordec was surprised, not at Kol's aggression but Gus's sharp response. He didn't need Gus to defend him against anyone, especially not this snotty boy.

'How'd you find the ship?' Kol said.

'I found it,' Mordec said.

Kol sniffed. But he took no more time than the two Hengists to make up his mind that he'd help to bring the 'half-ship' home.

'It will be the wonder of the Vikings,' he intoned. We'll go down in history for building it.'

'But *we didn't* build it,' Mordec said firmly without turning round, 'I told you—*I found* it.'

'In the winter nights in the mead halls,' Kol went on, as if too absorbed in his own dreams to hear what was said to him, 'the story-tellers will recite the Saga of Kol and his Half-a-Ship.'

'The Saga of Mordec and his Half-a-Ship,' Mordec said. 'Yes, I like the sound of it.'

Gus thought he'd have knocked Kol down if he'd been in Mordec's place. But Mordec only laughed.

surprise

The day of the launching of the new ships, fifteen days before the summer voyage was due to start, was a festive day. The men and older boys began gathering in the shipyard, on the harbour quay, on the beach and on the meadows well before noon, and the men started drinking at once. The women, wearing ribbons and flowers, came later with the younger children. Fires were lighted and meats were held over them on long sticks.

Girls clustered together and blew tirelessly on small shrill whistles made of hazel bark, until a grown-up arrived with a drum and a horn and told them to stop it. Prentice lads sang bawdy songs and danced with each other in a wild manner.

Warm days like this made the seafarers feel restless ever since the season of sailing had been changed from winter to summer. They watched the shipbuilders climbing in and out of the new ships with growing impatience, and when Olaf the Shipbuilder climbed down for the last time and called to his lads to carry the tools away, a cheer went up from Hakon the Tanner. Sitting on the grass with his big wife Tove beside him and a cask between his feet, he was wildly drunk.

'Let'sh go tomorrow,' he shouted, 'and shtart the shummer early.' He roared with laughter and those near him joined in. When he'd finished laughing he bent his head back, lifted the cask and poured a stream of ale straight down his throat. Some of it ran over the two braids of his yellow beard and down his chest. He wiped it away and dried his hands in his wife's hair. Tove let him, took no notice. She was noble-minded, full of heroic dreams. In her youth she'd believed that Hakon was a born hero. Now her hopes lay with her son Gus.

A horn-blast and drum-beat silenced everyone and they looked up to the low cliff on one side of the bay where the priest stood. He'd been an imposing figure in his prime, but now he was shorter and stouter. He hoped that when he stood up there he'd still seem tall to those below. He wore yellow robes, his beard hung to his golden girdle, and a gold disc on his forehead reflected the sinking sun. He raised his arms and called upon Odin and Thor in a quavering voice to watch over the new ships and guard the warriors on their voyage to the western isles. The folk below were beginning to wonder how much longer this would go on when he stopped abruptly and peered at something out at sea, shielding his eyes with both hands. They all turned that way and soon made out a small ship coming shoreward down the glittering path of the setting sun.

It was a finely streamlined craft with a high slender prow but no mast. It was rowed with rough sticks and planks which rose and fell so higgledy-piggledy that it couldn't advance in a straight line but zig-zagged like a wolf on a scent-trail.

Then the men saw that their sons were the rowers: Olaf's son, Hakon's son, Hauk's son, Harvald's son, Gunnar's son, Knefrod's son … Ten boys in all were rowing clumsily for the shore. Olaf the Shipbuilder was the first to overcome his surprise, and being instinctively practical when it came to the safety of ships he quickly took charge of the landing.

'That's far enough!' he shouted. 'Don't beach her! Get out, hold her!'

He circled his arms in the air to get them jumping overboard as he ran into the sea to meet them. He saw his own son stand up in the ship and wave and grin.

'Out, out!' he bawled, and young Olaf obeyed. The others followed, dropping over the side to stand in the shallow water. Big Olaf waded out to them, and behind him with a whoop of excitement his prentice lads came splashing, to have a close look at the ship and help to bring it in. They beached it safely, lodged it between two of the new ships, like a foal between mares.

When at last, to repeated cheers and a rolling of the drum, the new ships were launched one by one, bonfires were lighted. The flames leapt high but were paled by the level beams of the sun. Then attention was turned again to the small ship, and even the priest came to take a closer look. But no one was as pleased with it as Olaf the Shipbuilder. He examined every part of it, and only hours later began to ask his son the questions that the boys had been expecting.

That night when their son was asleep the Shipbuilder's wife Brynhild said to him, '*You* built it, didn't you?'

'Long ago. When I was a prentice lad. It was my masterpiece.'

'Will you tell them?'

'Maybe one day. I'll keep them wondering awhile. If they want to think it was made by magic, let them. Magic or something must have kept it safe all these years from damp and worm and marauders. There's not a hole in it anywhere, only rust, and some of the caulking needs to be redone. D'you know, even the lashings of the lowest strakes are still firm! If it wasn't kept by magic or the gods, how did it happen that neither time nor vermin split them with their teeth?'

foal of the foam

Big Olaf took great pleasure in working on the small ship with the same loving care he'd put into the making of it long ago for the son of a rich man. He showed the boys how to tar wool for the caulking and press it into gaps and spaces which at first they'd swear did not exist at all. He fashioned the pine mast, and with the boys' help planted it in the oak box amidships. All the boys worked long hours on making real oars, but only those from the hands of Little Hengist were usable. Thralls and prentices shaped the rest.

Gunnar's father the Sailmaker gave the boys a sail, trimmed down from a larger one. Mordec, Gus, Eric and Big Hengist carried it to the ship, and Gunnar showed them how to fix it to the cross-beam, spread it, reef it, furl and lash it. They learnt how to steer, and with oars of properly graded lengths how to row in unison. When a steady wind took them to the near islands, boys stood on beaches to watch them sail by.

'What's your ship's name?' one of them called.

'Foal of the Foam,' Mordec shouted back, the name popping into his head just at the moment he needed it.

'Who says?' Kol demanded.

‘I, Mordec the Finder,’ Mordec replied.
‘Kol turned to Gus. We weren’t asked,’ he brayed.
‘He found it,’ Gus said. And Kol frowned.

the old armourer

Horsa's grandfather Harvald had for many years made weapons and armour for Eyiolf the Bald, the Terror of the North, East, and West. Eyiolf had had enough sense to keep a good craftsman in good heart, and had rewarded Harvald with land, herds, and gold, but had also threatened him that if he were ever to make weapons and armour for any other man, he could expect *the worst*.

By the time Eyiolf the Bald died in battle and his soul departed to the Hall of the Heroes, Harvald had grown old in his service. His beard was long and straggly, his hair streaked with grey, and he had few teeth left. But he was still strong and his hands worked as well as ever.

When he got home after fleeing Eyiolf's fortress shortly before it was sacked, he sat on a stool beside his square hearth in the middle of his house and said to himself, 'Why should I risk the wrath of the soul of Eyiolf? Does anybody know what power the soul of a dead hero might have to punish a living man? Nobody knows. It may be he could do *the worst* to me yet so I'll take no risk.' He looked up at his smoke-blackened roof-beams, folded his arms, stretched out his legs, and winked at nobody. 'Eyiolf said I must not make armour and weapons for any *man,* but not a word did he say against making them for dolls, to amuse the gods.'

So in the big shed that stood between his house and his cow-barn he turned out weapons and armour that anyone could see at a glance were too small for any *man.* He put them on straw figures with painted faces. Once in a while he would bring a few old cronies home with him from the mead hall to see his handiwork.

'Meet Sigmund and Sigvat Straw,' he'd say, or 'Harald Lighthead' and 'Edvald Brainless'.

And his friends, being in high good humour with the glowing mead inside them, would talk and joke with the dolls. Once a farmer who'd drunk too much kissed a pair of the painted lips, which made Harvald think he should make some pretty girl dolls, and children too.

Next he made the figures move by using weights and ratchets, pendulums and coils. When Horsa came with nine other boys to his workshed he set his straw warriors to do battle with each other, lifting shields and wielding swords. Little Hengist wanted to know how it was done, and the old man showed him.

'Now that's enough.' the old man grunted. 'If there's nothing more you want, get along back home. I've work to do.' And he went to his workbench, picked up a chisel and started honing it.

'Grandad,' Horsa said, 'we need armour and weapons. Then we can sail in our ship with the fleet and raid England.'

'Mm-hm,' Harvald said, seeming to give all his attention to the work he had in hand. 'Why ask me? Ask you father.'

'I did and he said no.'

'Then he won't want me to give them to you, will he?'

'He didn't say.'

'You want to wound and kill?'

'Oh yes!' they said.

The old man laid down his work and looked from one to the other of the eager faces round him.

'Then by Thor I will!' he crowed, banging his fist down on the bench and laughing.

None of the boys, not even Mordec, could see the joke.

in the mead hall

On the night before the start of the westward voyage, the men gathered as they always did in the mead hall. They drank to a successful season of trading and plundering. Only the farmers grumbled a bit as they always did about the shortage of good land for crops and grazing, and one of them announced that he was thinking of taking his family with him to England next year and never coming back again.

At one or another table a song broke out, and the laughter got louder.

'Time for a story!' Hakon shouted. He wiped his mouth with the whole length of his forearm.

In the middle of the long room a chair had been placed for the Skald. There he seated himself in solemn dignity, and in his firm clear voice recited a story of a dragon, a sorcerer and a troll, and a hero who vanquished them in perilous struggle. When it was done and the rowdy applause over, he said, 'I have composed a new poem for you who are gathered in this hall.' And he recited these lines:

Not of battles I sing now. Mere boys are my heroes.
The children of warriors were warriors in wishes,

But their fathers forbade them to follow the longships.
Unless in a half-ship, unheard of in story.

Helpless to hew and build, but with hearts hoping,
Some lads spoke of spells, sorcerers' magic.
But Kol searched keenly, hied over heathland,
Fast-footed it daylong through tall fir forests,
Alone with his longing to follow the longships,
Finding at last an old shipyard forsaken,
And there awaiting, a wonder from Woden,
Reward for his wishing, a half-long longship.

He fetched his fellows, told not the fathers,
Led the bewildered boys back to the half-ship.
Astonished they stared, dumbstruck by the treasure,
Then strongly they strove to launch it on sea-wave.

When folk were feasting round fires on the seashore,
And the priest prayed, begging blessing of Woden
On the new ships, new steeds of the sea-fields,
All that were gathered there thrilled to a wonder.
Out of the sun-disc, straight down the sun-path,
Came a craft half the length of a longship,
Flying fast to the fjord, full of their sons,
To beach with the new boats braced between bonfires.

Never before borne to ear of the hearer
Was legend of lads lone-sailing a longship,
Voyaging to vanquish, as if full-grown Vikings.
The reward is the wave-ride and its dangers,
May they be brave ever, bold as their fathers.

The warriors cheered. Their boys' exploit had brought them fame. The Skald would tell this story in many halls and other story-tellers would learn it from him. When his plates were passed round they heaped coins on them. They knew that whatever they parted with tonight they'd recover many times over in their raid on England.

mordec enraged

When Horsa stood before his father in his new armour and holding his sword, Harvald son of Harvald showed no surprise.

'So your grandfather gave you arms and armour,' he said. 'Did he give it to all of you?'

'All ten of us.'

'Very well then, the ten of you will voyage with us to England. You'll sail in Foal of the Foam.'

Olaf's father said much the same. He felt he had no choice but to honour his promise, though it had been made as a joke.

Other fathers followed their lead. But Estrid refused to let Mordec sail.

'It's different for the other boys,' she said. 'They'll have their fathers with them.'

Hauk was not going on the voyage this year. His trade in honey and mead was doing too well to leave it now.

'Don't be cross about it, Mordec. You'll be voyaging soon enough—next year, most likely.'

'I'm not cross because of that,' Mordec said, 'I'm only shattered.'

'Well, that's not too bad. What is it you're cross about then?'

'Cross? More like furious, enraged.'

'But what about?'

'About what the Skald recited in the mead hall last night. They're all talking about it. And Kol's going round smirking. But it wasn't Kol who found the ship. *I* did.'

'It's true,' Estrid said. 'Kol must have lied to the Skald. I was also cross about it.'

'I still am,' said Hauk.

'I'll set the bees on him,' Mordec threatened. 'And on the Skald. He prophesies great things for me and then takes away the one great thing I've done. He's lost his *second* sight now too!'

'Was it great, what you did?' Estrid asked. 'Lucky is what I'd call it.'

'Still, it was me, not Kol. And the Skald seems to think it's great, so he ought to praise me and not Kol. And on top of all that Kol's going to sail and I'm not.'

'It *is* a bit much to swallow,' Hauk said, looking at his wife. 'Mordec, go and see how the loading of the ships is getting on. I need to talk to your mother.'

Mordec went. But Estrid said, 'I'm not listening, Hauk.'

'Then I'll just talk to myself.' Hauk picked up a tin plate and told his reflection, 'That boy has had a raw deal. If it hadn't been for him there'd be no small ship for the boys to sail in. But he gets no credit for it, and what's more, he alone of all those who brought it home is not allowed to sail in it. From now on he'll believe there's no justice in this world.'

'He'd be right,' Estrid said, trying not to laugh.

'And do you know,' Hauk went on, 'I'd even asked Olaf the Shipbuilder and Harvald the Armourer to be guardians of the boy while they're abroad. Silly of me to think I could persuade my own wife to change her mind!'

Estrid threw up her hands and said 'I give up. You're right. We can't let them treat our son like that. If you're sure Olaf and Harvald will look after the boy as if he were their own—well then—'

the sailing

The loading of supplies was nearly finished, and the men stood with their wives and children, ready to say their farewells and embark. There were aching heads among those who'd drunk most heavily the night before, but their owners knew better than to complain to their wives who would only say 'I told you so'.

A row of boys was waiting too, tall and short, fat and thin, all wearing helmets and bearing shields and weapons. The tall one at the end of the row looked through a pair of glasses.

'You look stupid wearing glasses when you're in full armour.'

It was the boy standing next in line who spoke, his mouth twisted in a sneer.

'You know,' Mordec said, 'there's only one thing you could tell me that I'd believe.'

'What's that then?' Kol asked with the sneer still on his face.

'That you're a liar,' Mordec said.

Kol stepped out of line and pointed his sword at Mordec. Mordec raised his. Old Harvald had given the boys hasty lessons in the use of their short swords, and now these two looked so truly threatening that the others took a step away from them, except Horsa who

29

was schooled in the arts of combat. With his own sword he struck theirs aside, first Kol's, then Mordec's.

'Vikings don't fight each other when they go raiding,' he said.

And slowly, looking warily at each other, the two lowered their sword-arms.

'We sail!' came the cry, and men climbed into the ships, hung their shields over the sides, unfurled sails, and put out the oars. Two hundred men in eight ships.

When the boys, with fast-beating hearts, were seated in their own half-ship, Big Olaf came and tied a rope round its prow which curled over like a frond of bracken but had no carved dragon-head on it as the others did.

'Ah no, Dad!' young Olaf wailed. 'We're not going to be towed, are we? We've got a sail and proper oars.'

Big Olaf waded to his own ship, Elk of the Seawaste, to attach the other end of the rope to its stern. Then he came back to them.

'It's just for the start,' he said. 'If the weather stays good you can try keeping up with us on your own. Only at night I'll tie you again. Which one of you is captain?'

'I am!' Olaf, Gus and Mordec shouted.

'You can't have three captains,' Big Olaf said, laughing. 'And I don't suppose you need one. You'll be taking your orders from me.'

The ships departed, Elk of the Seawaste and Foal of the Foam last. The seafarers kept their hands on the oars and only the folk on the shore waved.

Estrid held Hauk's arm tightly. Two other fathers who were staying behind shouted last minute advice to their sons, their voices floating a name on the breeze, 'Hengist …! Hengist …!'

And Grandfather Harvald watched from the cliff, laughing to himself.

raiders

A brisk wind whipped up a choppy sea and blew spindrift into the seafarers' faces. Mordec's spectacles were soon opaque with salt water-drops so he took them off. Big Hengist was sea-sick and for half an hour hung over the side, crying out between bouts of retching that he wished he hadn't come, he'd rather be anywhere but in a ship, and he'd never eat anything again. Olaf told Horsa that he hoped they'd meet a foreign ship and his father would let them attack it.

'Do you know how to attack another ship?' Horsa asked him.

'There can only be one way,' Olaf said. 'You …'

'Yes?' Horsa said.

Olaf fell silent.

'So you don't know. And let me tell you something. Any captain of a foreign ship who sees us coming will melt away like snow on fire.'

'But if a whole foreign fleet …'

'I hope not,' Horsa said. But in case Olaf was about to accuse him of fearing battle, and because he really was looking forward to using his new weapons, he added, 'We'll fight when we get to England.'

The wind dropped and the sea calmed soon after sunset. The boys fell asleep. Lucky then that their ship was tied to a bigger one or they would have drifted far from the fleet and even perhaps into a sea-dragon's maw. Before dawn Mordec opened his eyes when the northern lights were rippling down the sky. The others slept through the short night and into bright morning. Big Hengist found that his appetite had returned.

'This is a great life,' he said, and added that no real Viking had ever been put off by a spot of sea-sickness.

Through the second day and night they were smoothly blown west and south-west, and while they were breakfasting on cold fried kippers and flatbread on the third morning, the first of the western isles drifted by on the horizon in a haze. Gulls screamed, sheering on wind-currents, and porpoises raced beside the ships.

They'd no sooner finished eating than the wind dropped and Big Olaf hailed them and shouted an order to 'row and keep close'. He let out most of the tow-rope until the greater part of it lay invisible in the water, then he shouted through cupped hands that if it tautened so that his ship felt the weight of theirs, he'd know they were slacking at the oars. Eager to prove themselves the boys rowed until they were sweating and aching.

Eventually a breeze arose and filled the sail so the oars could be shipped, and thankfully they rested their arms and backs, doused the blisters on their hands with brine. The fresher wind blew them swiftly towards England.

Kol, clinging to the prow, honked 'Dragon!— there, there …' but no one leapt up. Two or three half rose, gazed in the direction Kol was pointing and saw only the broken sunlight on the water.

Mordec was reclining in the stem, slicing a thick sausage into ten equal pieces. He said with a noisy sigh of mock patience, 'We must all try to remember that Kol just can't help telling lies. He tells them as easily as a porpoise turns over.'

Kol, with the wind in his ears and his attention on the dragon-hiding sea, heard neither these words nor the burst of laughter from Big Hengist, who was keeping a watch on the sausage.

True excitement raised the boys to their feet when at last the men shouted 'Land ho!'

They saw flat islands floating on either side, separated from each other by water-courses as narrow as threads, except for the river—the river Nijn they were to learn it was called—up which they drifted between low green banks, on and on as if bound for the land's heart.

Beyond the islands were water-meadows, and when they gave way to endless fields of sopping grass, the sails were furled. Boys leapt to lash their own, not waiting for Big Olaf to shout an order. Others plied the oars, and Big Olaf shortened the tow-rope, letting it straighten or droop in the air, guiding, not pulling, the small ship to the river-harbour.

They docked it themselves in line with the other ships at a wooden landing-stage.

When all had been made fast by hawsers tied to stout posts, the men donned their helmets and leapt ashore, and ran shouting and laughing, brandishing swords and shields.

The boys did the same, ready to storm the defending enemy.

Mordec thought, 'I shall fight fearlessly and win, like Alexander.'

But no enemy appeared, and on they ran through long grass towards a cluster of small houses. They reached the doors, and still no defenders came out to confront them. The boys stood holding their swords upright, pressing their shields to their sides, their eyes fiercely or fearfully glaring about from under the rim of their helmets. No hearth-smoke rose from the houses. No herds grazed near by. Had even the animals fled in fear of the invaders?

Mordec felt the very emptiness to be threatening.

'They must've all run away when they saw us coming,' young Olaf said to his father.

'Who d'you mean?' Big Olaf asked, removing his helmet. 'You can take your armour off now.'

'What if they suddenly attack us, Dad?'

'Who?'

'The people who live in these houses.'

'No one lives in these houses. Only us. They're our houses. This is where we live when we come here.'

'Aren't they—weren't they—I mean, who built them?'

'Oh, English folk *built* them. But we took them over.'

'Didn't they mind?'

'Who? The English? Of course they minded. They didn't give them up easily, you know. We had to burn down a house or two before they understood we meant business.'

'Where'd they all go?'

'Not far. You'll see them. They'll be coming soon with food and stuff to trade.'

'Horsa, Mordec, all of you, come over here.'

It was Harvald the Armourer calling them.

'This is the biggest house and you lot can have it. See? Long benches … a good wide fireplace … pots and pans. Of course everything's very dusty. Get it cleaned up. And fetch water for yourselves and for me. I'll be in the house next door.'

Little Hengist mended a broken chain over the hearth and Mordec got the fire going. Horsa and Titch fetched water from the river. Gus, Eric and Kol dropped their stuff in heaps on the benches and went off, armed with their swords, to explore as much of England as they could before dinner. 'It's going to be funny with no mothers,' Big Hengist said.

'I don't know about mothers,' Gunnar replied from the doorway, 'but there's no shortage of women. Look.'

Mordec and the others went to look. Women and girls were approaching over a field to the south, a long straggling line of them. They carried pails and baskets.

'I think it's dinner coming,' Mordec said.

A chorus of hulloos brought the men out of the houses. They looked pleased to see the visitors. 'Hulloo, hulloo!' they shouted back.

Some of the girls, the ones least weighed down with burdens, broke into a run. They gathered in front of the boys' house, smiling and chattering.

Knefrod the Hunter made his way through the crowd to a plump young woman, put his arm about her waist and kissed her heartily on the lips.

Hakon put his arms round the waists of two at the same time, lifted them off their feet, spun round, and yelped. One of the youngest girls set down her basket, joined hands with Gunnar's big brother Egil and danced with him. There was a hubbub of laughter and chatter.

Olaf muttered to Mordec, 'They don't seem to be afraid of us, do they?'

'They don't seem to mind at all about being invaded,' Mordec agreed.

The girl who'd been cavorting with Egil said pleasantly, 'I was saying to Isolde only yesterday, it's getting so warm they'll be here any day now. Wasn't I, Isolde?'

'You was,' said Isolde, the plump young woman in Knefrod's embrace. 'Real pillage-and-plunder weather, you said. And so it is.'

More laughter, and the girls began to unpack their wares. Mordec walked about inspecting them. As he'd thought, it was dinner. There was milk, goat's cheese, flour, root vegetables, eggs, smoked hams, live chickens squawking and flapping in basket-work cages, bunches of dead rabbits stretched out long and thin, earthen bottles of ale sealed with wax, leather jugs of wine with tin stoppers. The men fetched bales and casks from the ships. Hakon set down a bundle of furs in the midst of the crowd and, laughing, cut the cords that bound it with his dagger. The girls took up the skins one by one and inspected them with solemn eyes and careful fingers. Two of the men set out small barrels of Hauk's honey—ten rows of ten, Mordec counted. Egil gave the girl he had embraced—Maisie was her name—a necklace of amber beads; Knefrod put a band of silver on the arm of Isolde.

When the girls had gone with their furs and honey, the men divided up the food, giving the boys their share. The live fowls were not handed out. Big Olaf released them into a mud-walled pen behind the biggest house and scattered corn for them. 'If you hear them getting very loud,' he told the boys, 'come and chase the fox away.'

That night the men drank much and slept soundly.

The boys tasted the ale and wine and talked until late. Eric said that he and Gus had climbed a tree and seen the turrets of a castle to the north. Kol said he'd seen a lion.

'With wings?' Mordec asked.

'Yes,' said Kol.

'And was his tail a snake?'

'Yes.'

'Well, be very careful then. What you saw was the dreaded Lion of Loondal, and there's an old English tale that whoever sees it is doomed to fight it, and all but one man will be killed and eaten by it.'

Kol thought about this for a while. Some of the boys fell asleep. The rushlights burnt out. 'How d'you know?' Kol's voice suddenly demanded in the dark.

He listened for an answer, but either Mordec didn't want to say any more or he too was sleeping.

plunder

Next morning, a hundred of the men sailed on southward in four of the ships.

Most of the rest set out early on foot, armed.

'While we're gone,' Big Olaf told his son and Eric, the only boys who were up and about, 'Bodvar and Hrolf will stay here on guard.'

Bodvar and Hrolf were two of the Shipbuilder's prentices.

'Can't we come with you?' young Olaf begged.

'No.'

'What'll we do then?'

'Why don't you boys rustle up a few horses?'

'Where?'

'That way.' Big Olaf pointed. 'There's a village over there called Podthorpe Growl. About an hour's walk away. Go and look for them there. Maybe Egil should go with you.'

'No. We'll be alright. I promise. Don't make Egil come with us. We'll put on our armour and take our weapons.'

'That won't be necessary,' Big Olaf said. 'You'll find it easier to bring the horses home if your hands are free.'

When Olaf told the other boys what their mission was, a cheer went up.

'Our first chance for pillage and plunder,' Horsa said.

'My dad said we shouldn't take weapons.'

'But we must,' Gus said. 'Arm yourselves, everyone. And take rope.'

Looking serious so as not to show the excitement they felt, the boys put on armour and swords, and hung coils of rope on their shoulders.

When Mordec returned from a swim in the river he found them ready to go.

'Where are you off to?' he asked.

They told him.

'I think—' he began.

'You think too much,' Kol interrupted.

Mordec went on as if he hadn't heard, '—that if force is needed to get horses, they wouldn't send us for them, they'd go themselves.'

'This is our first raid,' Gus said. 'You coming or not?'

'He's scared,' Kol said.

'You can stay and make the dinner,' Big Hengist suggested, wistfully rather than mockingly.

'I'm coming,' Mordec said, and despite his opinion that weapons would not be needed, he strapped his sword to his side.

They set off, Gus leading the way. He took them over grass and through the thin margin of a woodland, where, looking deeper in among the trees, Kol announced that he could see a wild boar. Nobody believed him.

It took them less than an hour to reach the village of Podthorpe Growl. 'Line up in three rows of three,' Gus said when it came in sight, 'and follow me.'

They obeyed, since Gus seemed to know what to do and no one else did. Mordec stood quietly in the middle of the back row. Gus strode out in front, and the three rows advanced behind him. When he broke into a run, they did too. 'Swords,' he shouted as they came within twenty yards or so of the first house, and they all drew and flourished their weapons as they ran.

The villagers who were out and about—a woman carrying two pails of water, an elderly man crossing the dusty road with a load of straw on his back, a farmboy driving an ox, a small boy pursuing a gaggle of geese with a willow wand, and a white-bonneted housewife picking dust-wisps off a broom—looked round as the shouting began, but went on with what they were doing.

Mordec saw a few faces appearing in the windows of the houses they passed; an old woman, a girl, a mother with a baby, all calmly watching the invaders pounding by with raised swords.

'They've sent boys this time,' the woman with the pails called to the straw-carrier, and he turned slowly with his cumbersome load to stand in the way and face the onslaught. He waited until they'd arrived within a few feet of where he stood, then he nodded at Gus and sang out, 'G'morning!'

Gus stopped, raising his left hand to stop the others.

'G'morning,' he replied, and frowned in what he hoped was a menacing manner.

'What now?' Mordec wondered, and let his sword hang at his side.

'They're down there,' the straw-carrier said, tossing his head to indicate the other end of the village.'

'Who are?' Gus asked. Did the man mean that fighters were waiting for them down there?

'The horses,' the man replied in a matter-of-fact tone. 'They're all ready and waiting.' He nodded affably and went on his way.

Gus glared after him, then brought his feet together, brandished his sword over his head to marshal his platoon, and 'Follow me!' he commanded. He strode forward and the boys came after him; but feeling a little foolish, they broke ranks and spread out in a straggling line across the road, waving their weapons about as if they were only meant for slashing at the hollyhocks which grew beside the cottage doors.

At the far end of the village was a field roughly fenced with posts and logs, and in it horses were grazing. Some, Mordec noticed, were grey and drooping with age, others barrel-bellied or ribby. A few looked strong enough, but none would have fetched much of a price in the market.

Gus set Horsa and Kol to guard the gate while he and the others roped the strongest-looking animals. 'We'll lead these out,' he said, 'and maybe the others will follow. When we're clear of the village, we'll ride. Eric, if you stay behind you can keep the stragglers going.'

Mordec wandered off on his own. 'Somewhere here,' he thought, 'they've got the good ones hidden away.' And he soon found that he was right. Through a chink in a barn wall he glimpsed three well-groomed horses such as any warrior would be proud to ride, and two piebalds each strong enough to pull a cartful over a mountain. He walked on, and came to a path that led to the banks of a stream. On the other bank rose a hump of rough grassland, the nearest thing to a hill in this flat country, and as he looked a horse came up from the far side, galloping. It stopped when it reached the low summit, and turned as if it had come there to survey all the land below. As it was above him it seemed to Mordec to have amazing height. Its colour was impressive too, a shining blue-black. The long dense hair of its mane and tail blew in the breeze.

'*Yes!*' was all he said, and as the beast lowered its head to crop the grass, he moved quietly away. It would take more than one of them to capture this proud creature.

He didn't tell the others about the horses in the barn. Hiding them away, he thought, showed the farmers' good sense. But they hadn't tried to hide the black one. 'The king of horses,' he told Gus. 'Let's go quietly.'

They crossed the stream well below the hump of land where the beast had been grazing, crept along the far bank, and came upon it. It was standing in the shallow water, drinking. It raised its dripping muzzle and looked at them with fierce eyes. Gus seized the moment to fling a wide loop of rope over its splendid head. At once it reared, flared its cavernous nostrils, snorted, and bared its teeth. Its hooves pawed the air before they crashed down, raising a drenching splash.

The boys hung on to the rope, though the beast reared again and brought its hooves down hard again.

'It may be wild,' Mordec gasped out, straining every muscle against the pull of the horse's neck. 'If it is we'll have trouble taming it. Watch out!' The horse reared again, and this time the boys flung themselves sideways to escape the descending hooves. But they didn't leave go. They were testing their strength against the beast. It was Mordec who suddenly understood that it wasn't trying all that hard to get away, and if it wanted to could easily have fled. Then either the rope would have been pulled out of their hands, burning the skin off if they'd clung too hard, or else they would have been dragged through the water, over the stones and across the common. At once the question formed in his mind—why didn't it? And the answer came: the beast was playing with them.

It proved to Mordec that he was right by suddenly standing still, then following them when they tugged quite gently on the rope.

'Will you try to mount it?' Mordec asked.

'Not this one,' Gus said. 'It'll have to be tamed first. But we'll take it. It's the only really good one.'

They both hung on to the lead-rope and when they rejoined the others on the edge of the village the boys cheered them or the horse. Gunnar and Titch were mounted and starting off in front. Eric brought up the rear on a fat, long-haired pony. The others led their beasts. The black came quietly, moving with the rest.

'Let's keep it in the middle,' he said to Gus. 'I don't think they meant us to have this one. They don't mind about the others I guess, but this should have stayed out of sight. They might try and take it back.'

'Then we'll fight them,' Gus said, full of bravado.

'Let's just keep moving,' Mordec said.

'It'll be mine,' Gus said.

'I don't think it'll ever be anybody's. Not if it doesn't want to be.'

'Mine,' Gus repeated. 'I'll keep it for myself.'

He held on to the rope tightly, hardly daring to hope that they would cover the whole distance without the beast asserting its will and escaping. But the horse did not pull back, or rear, or in any way resist the lead. It trod on quietly and firmly among the sorry old nags and misshapen ponies.

'When it wants to go,' Mordec said, 'it'll go.'

The horses were ridden, led, driven into the field south of the Viking village. Bodvar and Hrolf left the game of hnefatafl they were playing in the shifting shade of an elder-tree and went to see to the hobbling of them. They recognized most of them, called some by names they had given them in past years. Only the black surprised them. 'That stallion—where'd you find him? How'd you get him here?' they asked, and Gus grinned with pride and said only 'Isn't it fine?' 'He is,' Bodvar and Hrolf agreed. Neither of them tried to hobble it.

The boys lingered in the field among the horses. But Mordec had been thinking that if he wanted good dinners he'd have to cook them.

He went to the chicken-run and chose two fat capons. He drew a line in the sand and pressed the birds' heads down until their beaks touched the line. There they remained motionless while he cleaned the chopping block which stood in one corner of the yard, and scraped the rust off the axe which had been left lying on the block since last summer. Then he fetched the birds one at a time, chopped their heads off and plucked them. On the way back to the house he saw that Gus was chasing the black horse round the field while the other boys cheered him on. But Gus gave up. At once the horse stopped and lowered his head to graze. Gus walked slowly up to it and put a hand on its handsome neck. Seeing Mordec leaning on the fence he called out to him breathlessly, 'It won't let me mount.' Mordec was not surprised to hear it. He went to cook the dinner, and Big Hengist was the first to come away from the field, drawn to the house by his nose. The others soon followed.

They sat on the ground in front of the long house to eat the chicken stew. Gus had finally torn himself away from the stallion, leaving it grazing peacefully among the other horses. Bodvar and Hrolf came to join the boys, uninvited. Spoons were working busily when the sound of galloping hooves made them all look up. The black horse was pounding towards them, and someone was riding it, leaning over its neck. Men and boys flung themselves, rolling or leaping, out of the way. An ale jug was knocked over, and pigeons hanging about the dining place scattered in a flap of wings, leaving a drift of lost feathers. 'Odds-bods! Who's that on my horse?' Gus cried out. Looking after the retreating stallion they saw that the rider was a boy, dressed in buckskin from cap to shoes. Keeping his head well down, the boy clung to the neck as the beast plunged on, making for a narrow section of the river just north of the village. It leapt, showing the astonished boys the underside of its hooves, landed on the far bank, sprang on with a backward spurt of small stones, and plunged towards a thick wood.

'That snake's gone and stolen my horse!' Gus shouted. 'The low-down thief!' He ran after the vanishing horse and rider bawling, 'Come back or I'll hunt you down and kill you!' On the river-bank he stopped. Even at its narrowest it was still too wide for a boy to jump across. He came back heaving with anger. 'I'll find him, I'll get my horse back, and I'll chop him up,' he vowed, and he stood in the middle of the lane looking northwards although the horse and rider were no longer in sight.

The rest of the men returned before sunset, bringing nothing with them that the boys could see. The horses pleased them greatly. 'Well done,' they said, and asked no questions about where they'd been found. Gus told them that the best horse was the one that got away. His father Hakon guffawed. Big Olaf said, 'To lose only one is not bad. They may try and get some more back, but only after dark.'

'We'll ride them tomorrow,' Harvald the Armourer said. 'We've a long way to go.'

'And what about us?' Eric complained to his father, Svend the Dyer. 'We got them, we should be allowed to ride them.'

'Get some more,' Svend said, throwing up his arms. 'The land's teeming with herds of wild ponies. If you get the wild ones nobody comes and steals them back from you.'

The village was quiet, the boys asleep with their door open, when again hooves came thundering past the houses. Mordec woke to the sound, sat up and listened. He heard something hit the roof and a moment later a flaming torch flew in through the doorway and knocked against the log-pile beside the hearth. He shouted, 'Fire! Wake up! Fire! Get out of here!' Boys opened their eyes, bewildered, but were fully awake in seconds. They shook the others who were still asleep and yelled, 'Get up, get out!' Kol was the first through the door. They all went staggering out, safe from the fire but coughing as smoke thickened and spread through the house. The thatch was burning briskly and the log-pile had caught.

The noise of the galloping horse had brought the shamed watchmen running, and the shouts of the boys roused the other men. A line was formed from the river to the house and buckets of water were passed from hand to hand. The fire inside was soon put out, but stacks of thatch came flaring down from time to time and started it up again. When finally all the flames were extinguished, the walls still stood, streakily blackened. Most of the things belonging to the boys were saved, though many were charred and most were drenched. And the floor was a pool of water reflecting the waxing moon, as the roof had been burned away.

'That boy did it,' Gus informed everyone. 'I know he did. The snake who stole my horse.'

'Some snake, though,' Mordec said admiringly, 'to ride that horse. And get past the guard.'

'And he dared to attack *us* with flaming torches!' Gus said.

The boys dozed on the grass until sun-up. They saw the men trotting off on the stronger horses. Some returned an hour or so later behind a line of English labourers whose nag-drawn cart was laden with tools and new thatch. The boys' house was roofed again by sundown. But the boys had a dull supper of bread and boiled turnips.

maelstrom

'Mordec! Wake up! Come with me.'

Mordec opened his eyes. Gus, fully dressed, was shaking him. 'What is it?' Mordec asked, fumbling on the shelf above his head for his glasses.

'Come,' Gus said. 'I've seen my horse.'

'What d'you want me to do?'

'You'll see.'

He woke Eric and Gunnar too, and the three of them put on clothes and shoes. Gus hung a coil of rope on his shoulder. Moving about they disturbed some of the other boys but only Titch opened his eyes. He shut them again and went back to sleep.

Mordec felt the chill of the morning and saw the very crack of dawn, a gold streak where the sky touched the water-meadows. Gus led them through grass and nettles to a thicket-hedge. He knelt and peered through, and the others did the same. On a small field they saw the black horse grazing.

'Look,' Gus said softly, 'there it is. I'm gonna get it back now. Eric, you come with me. Mordec and Gunnar, keep watch. If you see that boy coming, whistle.' Gus and Eric dragged themselves through a gap in the hedge and made their way stealthily towards the horse. It raised its head from the grass, snorted and flicked its ears.

'It knows they're there,' Gunnar whispered. But the horse put a leg forward, stretched its neck, and started cropping again. The stalkers separated from each other, Eric to move round behind it, keeping his distance, and Gus to approach it with a looped end of rope in his hand.

'I'm going after them,' Gunnar said, and pushed through the hedge.

Mordec was startled by a voice murmuring very close to his ear, 'Don't move!' At the same moment an arm went round his neck and he was held firmly against the person who'd spoken, someone who knelt behind him and thrust a very sharp-looking dagger in front of his eyes, knocking his glasses into a tilt. 'And don't make a sound.'

With the arm holding his head back, Mordec wouldn't have found it easy to make any sound louder than a strangulated gurgle, and it would be easiest as well as safest, he decided, not to try even that much.

'I'll take my arm away but my dagger will be pointing to the back of your neck, so stay quiet.' His head was let go. Don't turn round,' the voice went on, 'just stay where you are and look straight in front of you and if you're very lucky I won't cut your ears off.'

He didn't stir, not even to straighten his glasses. He saw Gus throw the noose—uselessly, for at that moment a piercing whistle sounded next to his ear which made the horse raise and turn its head towards the hedge where he and his captor crouched. It came trotting towards them, Gus running after it. Gunnar, who was in its way, leapt aside and tumbled over. When it stopped under a tree near the hedge, the voice behind Mordec shouted, 'If you touch him, I'll cut your friend's ears off.' Gus stopped, Gunnar stayed sitting where he was, and only Eric, not knowing what was happening, moved. He ran towards them calling, 'Have you got it?'

Mordec cleared his throat.

'Yes?' said the voice. 'What are you making a noise for? Think I don't mean what I say?'

'May I speak?' Mordec asked.

'What d'you wanna say?'

'I think you should know—they wouldn't mind if you cut my ears off.' But he laughed as he said it.

'They're snakes,' the voice said. 'Now get up, go and stand by my horse, and remember—I'm close behind you with my dagger.'

Mordec did as he was told.

'You over there,' the voice called, this time to Eric. 'Stop and listen.'

Eric stopped, more in surprise than fear.

'Odds-bods!' Gus exclaimed as Mordec and the other emerged through the gap in the thicket. 'And we came without weapons.'

'Huh! Weapons or no weapons, you wouldn't stand a chance,' the voice said. 'Now listen. This is my horse. If you stay away from him I'll let you live. If you come near him again, I'll catch you one by one and cut you all up into bits.'

'O yeah? You and who else?'

'Me and my hundred knights.'

Gus thought about this. 'But it's my horse,' he said. 'You stole it from me.'

'No I didn't—you stole him from me.'

'We're the invaders,' Gus said. 'We take what we want until you defeat us in battle and drive us from your shores.'

'That's what I mean to do. Meanwhile, you won't have my horse.'

'I'm gonna take it right now. Try and stop me.'

'How are you going to take him? Can you ride him? I dare you to try and ride him.'

'I'll rope it and lead it. When it gets used to me I'll ride it.'

'He won't let anyone ride him but me. If you don't believe me, go on, try. I'm letting you.'

Feeling free from the threat of the dagger, Mordec edged away. He could see the boy who'd threatened him now. His build was sight, his eyes black-brown under severely straight eyebrows, and they had a proud fierceness in them, like the eyes of the horse. No hair showed under his buckskin cap, which, like his tunic, leggings, and boots, was wound about with rough string. The dagger was no longer visible. Mordec would have taken him for a poor forest boy, except that he seemed used to giving orders. And his age was hard to tell. He was almost as tall as Gus and himself, but his voice, though throaty, hadn't broken yet.

In response to the boy's challenge, Gus looked up at the branches of the tree, a stout oak. He climbed to a strong branch directly above the stallion. The boy went and stood in front of the horse and Mordec heard him say softly, 'Be still … wait.' And the beast stood still.

Gus lowered himself cautiously on to its back. 'There, you see?' He patted the splendid neck. 'Now tell me, have you given it a name?'

The boy ignored the question. 'Think you could stay on him if he galloped?' he asked.

'Maybe not—not until he's used to me. Gus. That's my name. He's Eric. And he's Mordec.'

The boy looked only at Gus. 'Can you ride? Can you gallop?'

'Sure.'

'Then I'll tell you what I'll do. I'll lend you a horse. Not him, another one, and I'll race you.'

'And whoever wins gets this one?'

The boy looked at Gus with narrowed eyes for a moment and then said, 'Alright.'

'And,' Gus said, 'can I also burn your house down?'

'No—why?'

'Wasn't it you came and torched ours?'

'Do you want to race or not?'

'What sort of horse will you lend me? Some winded old nag?'

'A good horse. Our next best after Maelstrom.'

'Maelstrom. So that's his name.'

The boy put his face close to Maelstrom's muzzle. 'Yes, but he's a wild horse. Wild and belonging to the wild. You couldn't tame him. Nobody could. He lets you ride him as a favour or not at all.'

'What a prize,' Gus thought, 'if I can break its will and make it obey me!'

'Get off now,' the boy said.

'No. Not yet.'

'Alright,' the boy said, and stepped back. '*Now!*' he shouted, and the stallion reared, throwing Gus to the ground.

He fell hard, the wind was knocked out of him, and the boy laughed. Gus got to his feet, gasping. But he would not admit even to himself that he couldn't break the horse to his will. When he'd recovered his breath he said, 'The race. When and where?'

'I'll show you,' the boy said, and started climbing the tree. 'Come on, follow me. You can see the place from up here.'

One by one they followed, and when they were all perched high in the oak, propped in a fork or astraddle a branch, the boy pointed into the distance. Mordec saw a road stretching north and south with no end in view and straight as an arrow's path.

'See?' the boy said. 'That's where we'll race.'

'Odds-bods!' Mordec said. 'Who made it?'

'The Romans. We'll race one mile along it. You agree?'

'What's a mile?'

'A Roman measurement. You'll know how long it is when you see it marked.'

So it was decided. Gus and the English boy would race each other for possession of the horse. The place, the Roman road. The time, noon tomorrow. The boy rode off on Maelstrom and Gus looked after him longingly. 'It's worth a try,' he said. 'If I don't win it I'll try taking it again—but next time I'll find somewhere to hide it.'

'It'll kill you. It's fierce,' Eric said.

'So am I,' said Gus.

the dragon and his thrall

Kol woke an hour or two after Gus, Eric, Gunnar, and Mordec had gone. He went looking for them and couldn't find them. He felt sure they were doing something specially interesting and deliberately leaving him out of it. He resented it. And he found it particularly galling that Gus should pick Mordec as one of his special friends and not him.

'I'll show them,' he thought. He would go off on his own, take his bow and arrows, and shoot something. A deer perhaps. Bring it back for dinner. Or maybe a dragon. In the best sagas, the heroes battled with dragons and defeated them. Of course he wasn't a full-grown hero yet, but perhaps he could find a smallish dragon to vanquish.

Off he went, and after an hour or so came to a forest of oak and ash, elm and lime, birch and beech in thick leaf. He moved stealthily from tree to tree, peering round the boles, expecting at any moment to see a dappled deer standing still while it browsed on the leaves of a sapling. Seeing ahead of him a clearing in which the sun struck down in shafts through the leafy forest-roof, he dropped to his knees and peered over a fallen tree. A rustling told him that something was approaching. But it couldn't be a deer. It was something that could speak. And there were more than one of them. A voice was answered by another voice. There they were now, emerging into the clearing, a man and a woman. Kol ducked his head. When he looked again, cautiously raising himself until his eyes were on a level with the top of the log, the two were sitting side by side with their legs stretched out, and a flask and a loaf were set on a red handkerchief spread between them.

'*Someone* knows where it is,' the man said. The words came fast and crisp. 'What we've got to do is find that Someone, and then we shall endeavour to persuade him that it is his *duty* to impart the information to us. That is *our* duty, and I for one will not shirk it.' He seized the flask, put it to his lips, drank, set it carefully down again, and wiped his mouth all the way round with his forefinger.

'After all,' the woman said, her lips pushed out, her eyes half closed, 'it's not in the public interest for resources to remain unproductive.' Then she too had a drink and wiped her mouth with the back of her hand.

The man was of middling height, dressed in a red tunic, a broad leather belt, green leggings and high buckskin boots. Tipped over his left eyebrow was a narrow green hat decorated with a long red feather. He had eyes as circular and shining as counterfeit pennies, ears like jug handles, a wide mouth and a bucket of a chin.

The woman was short and stout with a round head on a round body, like their loaf of bread. Her hair, cut short and straight to the lobes of her ears and across her forehead, was black, the little of it that showed under the grey woollen cap casing her head as snugly as an acorn cup. Her eyes were narrow and sleepy-looking, her cheeks as ruddy, round and creased as windfall apples. She wore a green woollen dress over a red petticoat. A thong of leather crossed her breast, wound about her middle and dangled a large iron key down the front of her skirt. Her stockings were grey circled with red. Her feet were thrust into wooden clogs.

'It's enough to make a decent person weep,' the woman complained sleepily, 'just to think of the sheer waste! There it lies, hidden away, year after year, while people are starving in Nimmerlinesland.'

'I have made it perfectly clear,' said the man, 'that I want none of it for myself. Not an ounce. It belongs to the people and should be restored to the people. What we must do is restore it to public ownership. Will you give me your full and unconditional support? Can I rely on you, Coo?'

'Haven't I proved my loyalty, Bill? It makes me sick,' the woman said, 'to think that there are people in this day and age who live in castles, feast day after day, when half the population of the world can't afford a simple roof over their heads.'

'Our task is to restore to the deprived what is rightfully theirs,' the man declared. 'We must reclaim it by whatever means is necessary.'

'We have a right—' the woman said.

'To the gold,' the man finished for her.

At that moment, Kol sneezed.

'The man leapt up. Who's there?' he called.

Kol stood up slowly. 'Only me,' he mewled, trying to smile placatingly.

The man eyed him warily. 'Only you? And who may you be?'

'Kol son of Knefrod the Hunter.'

'He's one of the invaders,' the man said to the woman. 'Now they're bringing their kids.' He turned his stare back on to Kol. 'What are you doing snooping about here?'

'Spying on us were you?' the woman said, thrusting her head forward.

'No, I—I'm only hunting.'

'Hunting what? Answer me!' the woman demanded.

'Deer. Or—or dragons.'

'Dragons eh? What d'you think of that, Bill? The lad's hunting dragons,' she said, and chortled, making a guttural 'hoo-hoo' sound.

'Come here, boy!' the man commanded.

Kol climbed over the log and sat on it, keeping his distance.

'So you're hunting dragons, are you?' Bill said.

'Not big ones,' Kol said humbly.

'Well, that's quite sensible,' the woman said.

'I've been called a dragon in my time, haven't I, Coo?' Bill said.

'And not without reason, if I may say so, Bill.'

'Why shouldn't you say so? It's true. D'you hear that, boy? I was nothing less than a dragon in my heyday.'

'You were a dragon?' Kol said. 'I don't understand. What d'you mean?'

'I don't think I can make myself any clearer,' Bill said. 'I *was* a dragon and now—well, I'm not exactly a pussycat—would you say, eh, Coo?'

'Oh you changed alright,' Coo said. 'You moved with the times.'

'Though I freely admit, I couldn't have done it without a little magic to help me.'

'Magic?' Kol said.

'I needed the touch of a magic wand,' Bill said. 'A certain wizard, you see, totally transformed my image. An enchanting human being, so to speak. "They must feel you are their friend," he told me, when he came to cast his spell. "You must *look* like the man you want to *be*. Put on warm, friendly colours. Learn to smile."' Bill demonstrated his smile, his lips parting to shape a wide bow, displaying more teeth than seemed common, all glinting like frost.

'So you were a dragon, and—,' Kol said, turning his eyes to the lady.

'You want to know what I was?' she said. 'I was the damsel he had in his power.' And she chortled again, her eyes becoming slits, and her mouth a funnel through which the sounds came out like coos, which might, Kol thought, explain her name.

'In thrall,' Bill said, and joined in the merriment with a short 'Ha, ha! Yeah. I had her in thrall.'

'Still have,' Coo cried out, and again she squeezed her eyes shut and gave herself up to another bout of pout-mouthed chortling.

Bill shut off his smile, sat down, and beckoned to Kol. 'Come closer, boy. Kol—is that your name? Come and share our small repast.'

Kol, not wanting to offend, crossed the clearing and sat down beside Bill. 'Some good fresh bread?' Bill said, and swung the loaf towards him. Kol's hand went up but the loaf was swung away before he'd touched it. 'What about a drink of home-brewed ale, then?' The flask flew towards him and away. 'No? Shout if you change your mind. Now tell me. You're a Viking boy, right? Hmm?'

'Right,' Kol said. 'And my father's a hunter, and—'

'He's over here too? For the summer?'

'Yes.'

'Raiding. Having a successful raiding season, would you say?'

'I don't know. I'm not sure.'

'What is it, would you say, that they like best about our country? Apart from the climate, I mean? Do they speak of that sort of thing at all, at home, in the frozen north, or on the high seas, in their ships?'

'O yes. They like tin.'

'And gold?'

'And gold. They come for tin and gold,' Kol said.

'Hah! Fancy that. Hmm. And do they usually find lots of it?'

'O yes, they do. Otherwise they wouldn't come again, would they? They'd go and look somewhere else.'

'That's right. That's very interesting. This is an intelligent boy, don't you think, Coo my dear?'

'I'll say he is!' Coo said, leaning back and looking at him with new respect.

'They must have a real talent for finding gold,' Bill said in a tone of warm admiration. 'A sort of instinct for knowing where to look. Tell me,' Bill put his head close to Kol's. 'Has your father said anything to you about *where* he plans to go looking? Whisper in my ear.' Bill twisted his head to one side to make his ear convenient to Kol.

'No,' Kol whispered, 'he hasn't.'

Bill straightened up. 'Well,' he said in his usual ringing tone, 'he'll be taking you with him one of these days, and then you'll know all about it.'

'I don't think he will. They never take us with them. None of us boys. Not even Mordec, and he's quite good at finding things, I s'pose,' Kol conceded.

'Mordec?' Bill said. 'Good at finding things is he? Tell me more about this Mordec. What's he found?'

'He found our ship. It's half-a-ship. And our fathers said we could come on a raid with them if we had our own half-a-ship to sail in.'

'And this Mordec found such a thing?'

'Well—yeah. He couldn't have got it to our beach without my help, but he pretends I had nothing to do with it.'

'That's a shame. A bad character, this Mordec.'

'He spoils everything. I wish he hadn't come. If he wasn't here I'd be having a really good time.'

'Hmm. Well, that's all very interesting. Eh, Coo?'

'Everyone's got troubles,' Coo said sleepily. Her head nodded forward and her eyes closed.

'I'm really glad you came to me with this problem of yours, Kol,' Bill said. 'Now, I wonder if I can't help you. I'm in the business of helping people. Coo and I—we care.'

'What can you do? You can't make Mordec go home. Unless—. D'you think this wizard could—er—.'

'Wizard? What wiz—O, him. No. It's—it's not in his line. But if this Mordec were to find something—something valuable, let's say—and not want to share it with you, maybe I could help you persuade him. Make him behave in a more friendly, giving manner. Selfish greed, Kol, is the curse of our age. People must be cured of it. Learn to share more, care more. Coo and I—we share. D'you see what I mean?'

'I'm not sure. I don't think Mordec knows where to find anything valuable round here.'

'Doesn't he really? Or is he just keeping it from you? Let me ask you this. Where has he gone to-day?'

'I don't know.'

'There you are. A secret expedition, hmm? Secret from you, that is. Did he go with the men?'

'No. He and some others left this morning before the men. I know because the horses were still in the field, and they mean to ride them somewhere every day. The best of them, anyway.'

But Bill was not listening. A far-away look had come into his wide-awake eyes. After a while he rose to his feet. 'Well,' he said, 'there's a lot we don't know, isn't there? But what I say is, it's all there to be found out. So now that we've become friends, let's keep in touch. Give me your hand and let me help you up. And if I may make a suggestion …' He put out a hand, but as Kol grasped it he let go so that the boy fell back again. Then Bill gave the boy's top-knot a sharp tug and Kol scrambled to his feet. His new friend put an arm about his shoulders, and leaning on him walked him about among the trees, talking confidentially. Coo took no notice. She lay sprawled on the forest floor, so fast asleep that a pair of thrush-es felt perfectly safe hopping on the handkerchief to peck up crumbs.

contest

When the news reached Reginald Earl of Linkard that there was to be a horse race on the Roman road, he declared he would be pleased to add a joust to the entertainment.

It was not often now that jousts took place, even in the richer courts. Since many small kingdoms, queendoms, and earldoms had fallen to the Viking invaders, there were few parts of England safe enough or courts rich enough to put on events such as fights-to-the-death between men or beasts. Earl Reginald's court was a rare exception. He even arranged entertainments for the common folk from time to time.

The Earl ruled his own territory both summer and winter, for he paid the Vikings to stay out of it. No stranger was allowed to enter the earldom bearing arms. But yesterday a knight had crossed the ford and even ridden over the drawbridge into the castle *fully armed.* He was therefore obliged by law to hazard his life in a joust-to-the-death with the Champion of the Castle, one Sir Cedric, a Linkardian knight who kept himself available for killing or being killed in return for a small retainer from the Earl. There'd been some uncertainty about the place for the fight, because the lawn of the tilting-yard within the castle walls had only just been replanted, and the tender grass-shoots were not to be trampled on. So when the news of the race had reached the court—'The Roman road!' exclaimed the Earl's Art Director, 'of course! Ideal for the joust. Why didn't we think of it ourselves?' The Earl declared himself pleased with the plan and at once gave orders that preparations were to be made just as they would have been within the castle; and, since the sport was to take place on the common highway, that the ordinary folk be let off work so they could come and watch the fun. It was this sort of thoughtfulness and generosity that made him much loved and honoured by his people, though he was nonetheless feared as a law-keeper.

Soon after sun-up carpenters, carriers and drapers were busy at the roadside under the Art Director's personal supervision. By the time the Viking boys arrived, a dais had been erected and chairs with tas-selled cushions placed on it under a canopy of yellow silk, and garlands of red and yellow rosebuds were in the process of being draped, and a man wearing glass-es was darting about and calling to a garland-hanger, 'Raise it higher! Bring it down! This way, no that way, hurry please!'

Drummers, flautists and trumpeters hung about in striped stockings, pointed shoes, and high collars, and among the gathering spectators, muffin-men and hawkers of live doves and toasted larks were shouting their wares.

All the boys except Big Hengist had set out before breakfast, with Gus in the lead, eager to start the day although they'd stayed up late the night before listening to a ridiculous story of Kol's about his meeting a dragon who'd been changed by a wizard into a man. 'You can still see the green scales on him in odd spots,' Kol had lied. 'Odd spots? Odds-bods!' Gunnar had teased him, but Kol stuck to his story, that he had met the dragon in the woods, and with him was his thrall. She hadn't been set free when the dragon was changed into a man. The wizard hadn't managed to do that. Anyway, the two of them just stayed together, and went about doing good. 'A dragon doing good?' Olaf said unbelievingly, and Mordec said: 'The only way a dragon can do good is by cutting himself up for the pot.' 'How d'you know dragon tastes good?' Big Hengist wanted to know. 'I don't,' was Mordec's reply, 'so I'd stew him and let you taste him first.'

At the Roman road the boys soon learnt that the crowd was not gathering only to see the race, but that the two knights were coming to try and kill each other, and the Earl and his daughter would watch both events.

The boy who had challenged Gus trotted up on Maelstrom with another horse on a lead, a bay gelding named Roman Ruin. By the time Big Hengist arrived after a proper breakfast, Gus was confidently galloping it along the road between the starting and winning-posts, but only once, no more, as he wanted to keep it fresh for the race.

The dais faced the road not far from the winning-post, and on either side of it, but well apart, were two small tall round tents, one white with a white flag on its peak, the other black with a black flag. The Art Director looked from one to the other and nodded with satisfaction. The first thing Mordec noticed about him was that he wore glasses, the only fellow glasses-wearer he'd ever seen except his dimly-remembered grandfather who'd come on a visit once when he was little. This man's were round, sturdily framed in some metal—tin, Mordec supposed—and painted ginger. The glass was so thick that the eyes seemed to bulge a little. Busy as he was, the man noticed the boy watching him intently. 'Hello there!' he called cheerfully from the dais, and swooped down on Mordec, smiling, one hand extended in greeting. He was clean-shaven and his straight ginger hair was combed smoothly over his ears. His nose was tipped up, his lips were soft and pink, his teeth white and even. He was dressed in a cherry-coloured surcoat with a wide silk sash. 'Mel de Gustybuss,' he named himself enthusiastically. 'Art Director to the Earl of Linkard. And you are—? Mordec? One of our Viking visitors? Enchanted. Got to rush. Hope we meet again.' And he was off, waving to the clumsy garland-draper and calling 'Hang on, I'm coming!'

Among the crowd Mordec saw some of the Viking men, among them Olaf's, Horsa's and Gunnar's fathers. There were not many left in the village now. Yesterday another forty-two had gone away on horseback, having first found themselves better horses than the boys had brought home.

Bodvar was one of those who'd stayed behind. There he was, standing in line with the muffin and bird vendors, selling little painted sticks. Mordec went to ask him what they were.

'If the black horse wins and you hold one of my long red sticks, I'll give you back the money you paid for it plus a pfenning. If you hold a short green one it means you backed the bay, and if that one wins I'll give you twice your money. Want one?' Mordec shook his head. 'Which have you sold more of?' he asked.

'The green,' Bodvar said, and winked.

'What about the joust?' Mordec asked.

'No one knows how good the white knight might be. Too high a risk.'

A mass of boys, Vikings among them, were clustered round a shepherd named Dick who told the strangers that he was trained to act as herald when there was 'jousting and such'. He also explained to them that it was easy to find a Roman mile on the Roman road, because the Romans had set milestones all the way along it. 'And ho and below!' he said, 'them milestones be *exackly one mile apart.* 'Ow they did it,' he mused, fingering his chin in wonder, 'no man of this world will ever know.'

'Weren't they men of this world?' Titch asked.

'The Romans? Men of this world? O no. They came from up there,' Dick said, jerking his shepherd's crook towards the clear blue sky, 'and back there is where they've went.'

Kol was wandering about on his own. He saw a muffin-man's tray set down and the man himself looking the other way, so he seized a muffin and was gone into the thick of the crowd faster than a frog can flick its tongue. He was munching happily and feeling safe when a hand came down on his shoulder. He started and looked round.

'Why, look who's here, Coo, m'dear! Hullo there! I say, is that fellow Mordec somewhere about? You could point him out to me.'

Kol was relieved to see that it was his friend the dragon and not the muffin-man. He's over there, 'he said. 'The one with the glasses on his face.'

'Na—that's Mel de Gustybuss,' Coo said. 'He's the Wizard, he is.'

The Wizard? Kol stared. The man Coo was looking at didn't seem much like a wizard as Kol had always imagined such a being from descriptions in stories. No dark robes. No high hat. No magic wand. And then there were the glasses.

'I don't mean him, I mean the boy—there.'

Bill and Coo stared long and hard at Mordec. They could tell at once that he wasn't their sort. Then Bill put a finger against his nose. 'Say no more. And you'll not be seen with us, right?' He squeezed Kol's shoulder, took hold of Coo's arm and strolled off with her.

Shortly before noon there was a bustle round the dais. The Earl and some ladies and gentlemen of the court were taking their seats.

'That's Earl Reginald,' said a stocky woman to Mordec and Gus, who were standing next to her in the crowd. She was shaped like one bundle of laundry on top of another, and carrying a sleeping baby, also bundle-like, in her short red arms.

Mordec thought the Earl was a pleasant-looking old man. He was dressed in a long red gown and a flat red hat decorated with a few pearls. Though his face was lined, his hair, neatly brushed and oiled, was still black. He smiled and waved at the crowd before sitting down. The crowd waved back and clapped their hands.

A very pretty girl of about sixteen sat beside him.

'That's 'is daughter, the Lady Jessica,' the stocky woman said. 'She's turned sixteen and not married yet. If she don't marry and have a son before the Earl dies, our land'll pass into the 'ands of strangers.'

The Art Director stepped on to the dais and took up a position on a comer from where he could survey the proceedings.

'That's Master Gustybuss. E's in charge of all them fol-de-rols 'n' thing-a-lings they 'ave to 'ave in castles.'

More gentlemen and ladies took their places, sitting or standing on the dais, and when they were assembled and looking expectantly towards the distant starting-post, a trumpeter stepped forward and blew a note on a long thin silver trumpet. Then Dick strode to the middle of the road, faced the Earl, took off his cap.

'The 'orses be ready, m'Lord,' he sang out.

'For the race or the joust?' the Earl inquired. He had a kind voice, quiet but clear.

'Which would you ladies and gennelmen 'ave first?'

'Let's have the joust, if the knights are ready,' the Earl said.

'Right y'are, m'Lord,' said Dick, bowing again. And off he went to look into the tents, first the black and then the white. Again the trumpet blew and the knights emerged, one in white armour and one in black. The boys had never seen armour so complete, covering not only the bodies but the limbs, the hands, the feet, and the faces. So heavy were the knights that four men had to help each of them into his saddle. Slowly they were lifted on to their mounts, black on black and white on white.

'The white one will win,' someone said, pushing in between Gus and Mordec. It was Gus's rival, the boy who was to race him for possession of Maelstrom.

'How d'you know?' Gus said. He tried to sound casual and steady, not wanting anyone, especially not this boy, to guess that his heart was beating fast and hard. The whole event with its unexpected splendour and the large crowd of watchers was making him feel tense and even a little nervous, a feeling he wasn't used to. He wished the Earl had asked for the race first. Impatiently, he beat his palm with the willow switch he'd cut to use as a riding crop. 'You're just saying that to sound clever,' he said provokingly to the boy.

'I'm not clever,' the boy said, his dark eyes moving from the black knight to the white and back again, 'but I know, because black knights never win.'

'On me RIGHT,' Dick roared, standing on the other side of the road from where the Earl and the Lady Jessica were seated on the tasseled cushions, 'the BLACK knight on the BLACK 'orse cap-harry-sohned in BLACK, the famous Champion of the Castle, Sir Cedric. On me LEFT, the WHITE knight on the WHITE 'orse cap-harry-sohned in WHITE, the unknown mis-cre-ant per-mitted by 'is Lordship in 'is just-ishi-arry cap-acity, to save or lose 'is life in mortal combat. May God decide the winner accordin' to 'is 'oly in-screw-tibble will.'

And Dick snatched off his cap and threw it down on the grass beside him.

The knights, each with his lance tucked under an arm and gripped in a gauntletted hand, urged their heavy mounts toward each other. After a few walking paces, they spurred them to a trot, then to a canter. When their poles were within reach of each other's breast-plates, each aimed his weapon at the heart of the other. The black knight missed his target and rocked in his saddle as the point of the other's lance slid off his armour. They passed each other, went on a way and turned their cumbrous steeds. The black knight dropped his lance, and took from the hand of an attendant a rod from which dangled a spiked ball on a chain. Again the combatants pounded towards each other. The black knight swung the ball on its chain round and round above his head and then reached out and aimed it at the white knight's helmet. But this time the lance of the white knight struck hard into the very centre of the black knight's breastplate and unseated him. The man in his metal casing came crashing down on the paving stones, gravel, pebbles, and scrubby grass of the road. He lay on his back, perfectly still. The white knight reined in his horse and rode slowly to his fallen foe.

'See, what did I tell you,' the boy said, and sighed loudly. Usually Sir Cedric wears white, and usually he wins, but he had to wear black today because the other knight wouldn't change.'

'Is he dead?' Mordec asked.

'Probably not. He may've broken a few bones,' the boy replied.

'But he's not moving,' Titch said.

'Could you move if you were locked into armour like that?'

'So why doesn't anybody come and help him up?'

'Because if he's not dead yet he's gotta go on fighting,' the boy explained patiently.

'He can't fight lying down like that!' Eric said.

'If he can't, the white knight will just kill him.'

'How?' Horsa asked.

'With his sword.'

Olaf was thrilled at the prospect. 'Does he have to? Is that the rule?' he asked.

'No, he doesn't have to. If he wants to he can let him off,' said the boy. 'But,' he added, 'that'd be very disappointing.'

And Olaf, Titch, and Horsa nodded their agreement.

The white knight dismounted slowly, unsheathed his sword with a flourish, put a foot on the chest of the black knight and slowly lowered the tip of his sword to the chain-mail round the fallen man's neck. The crowd, like one creature, drew in its breath. No cry rose from the man on the ground. Perhaps he was already dead. But no; the white knight removed his foot.

'I give you quarter,' the white knight shouted in a deep gloomy voice, 'instead of quartering you. That's my little joke, though heaven knows I'm not a joking man.' Then the black knight, after some twisting, kneeling, pushing and staggering, clanked to his feet.

'Let's see you then,' the Earl called.

Side by side the two knights faced the dais. With their feet planted firmly apart on the ground, they put their hands to their helmets. Sir Cedric was the first to bare his head, which he bowed as if apologizing for his defeat. But the Earl clapped, so the crowd did the same. Then the white knight lifted his helmet off and a gasp of surprise went up from the crowd because he was black. His face was very fine, his nose long and narrow, his brow high, his hair bushy, and his skin as black as pitch.

Gus smiled and knocked the boy beside him hard with his elbow. 'Ha, you see?' he said. 'The white doesn't always win.'

'Well done!' the Earl said, and threw a purse to the black man, who caught it, and holding it high, turned round to show it to the applauding crowd. 'Now,' the Earl said, 'you are free to enter my earldom fully armed.'

'It's us now,' the boy said. 'When we're mounted, we first go and show ourselves to Reggie and Jess, and then we race.'

Mordec held Roman Ruin's bridle, and Gus mounted.

The boy leapt on to Maelstrom. The contestants faced the dais, the horses tossing and shaking their heads. Lady Jessica, who was dressed in blue with a silver girdle and a small silver circlet on her head, came down, smiling, and handed up a favour to each of the riders; a long purple feather for Gus, a nosegay of ribboned field-flowers for the boy. Gus stuck his feather in the top of his boot and the boy pushed his nosegay down the front of his tunic as they walked their horses to the starting-post, where Dick was waiting cap in hand, ready to fling it down and start the race.

Mordec took up a position close to the winning-post and peered through his spectacles to make them out in the distance, the figures of the two riders, their horses pulling this way and that and stamping as they were reined back behind the starting line. He saw Dick fling down his cap. 'They're off!' the cry went up.

The horses sprang forward, Roman Ruin a fraction ahead of Maelstrom. Gus used his heels and willow-crop mercilessly, but the best he could do was stay neck and neck with the boy for some moments more. Then Maelstrom was out in front and coming on at such a speed that those seated on the dais could not help rising to their feet and cheering as he galloped by, eyeballs showing white, mane streaming in the wind of his own speed. 'Lily! Queen Lily!' the crowd yelled, and as Mordec wondered who 'Lily, Queen Lily,' was, Maelstrom shot past the winning-post and his rider rose triumphantly in the saddle, raised his arm, struck the air with his fist, and shouted in triumph. Seconds later Gus clattered up beside him and reined in a foam-lipped Roman Ruin.

'Well done, Queen Lily!' the voices went on yelling.

'You've won for me, Lily!' a man called out, brandishing a red-painted stick in the air.

Eric and Mordec looked at each other. 'Lily?' their expressions asked each other. Did the English give their sons the names of flowers? And call them 'Queen'? The boy was weaving and turning on his mount, this way and that, grinning widely. And as if to answer their unspoken question, he pulled off his cap and released a mass of waving dark brown hair. It fell about his shoulders, and only then it dawned on them that the rider who had beaten Gus was a girl.

'Odds-bods!' Eric exclaimed. 'But she rides like a man!'

Lily was riding back towards the dais where the ladies and gentlemen were still clapping. She dismounted and Lady Jessica came to talk to her. Gus walked up to them, leading Roman Ruin.

'Maelstrom can run!' he said to Lily. 'And you— you can ride.'

'You can too,' Lady Jessica said.

But Gus's eyes were fixed on Lily. 'Why didn't you tell me you're a girl?' he demanded.

Her smile vanished. 'Why should I? What difference does it make?'

Gus didn't answer. His gaze went to Maelstrom, and moved over him as if this was a long last look.

'He's best with you. He didn't like having me on his back. He's yours. And so's this one. Here, take him.'

'Roman Ruin's yours to use, if you use him well,' Lily said. 'Keep him while you're here.'

'You mean it?'

'Fetch him from me again next year. After that perhaps we'll be rid of you all.'

'I'll match myself against you again one day,' Gus said when he'd mounted the bay.

'Not for Maelstrom. He's mine forever. But there are even bigger things waiting to be fought over between you and me,' she said through her teeth, with sudden suppressed fury, glaring at Gus with her fierce dark eyes.

'It's hard to know,' he said, 'if you're friend or foe.'

'*Your* foe of course,' she replied.

Gus rode back to the village and the boys walked on either side of his horse, an escort of honor. Eric carried his riding-crop.

The new horse was put in the field with the others. It was understood that none of them should ride it unless Gus said he could.

Mordec asked for the feather which Lady Jessica had given him.

'What for?' Gus wanted to know.

'To write with.'

'I see—for showing off,' Gus said.

'Look who's talking.'

'You think I was—?'

Big Hengist interrupted with a blunt question. 'What've we got for dinner?'

a warning

Knefrod the Hunter came into the boys' house, where the stores were kept, to fetch a jug of wine. All the boys were there except Mordec, who'd gone fishing. They were arguing about what they should do that afternoon. Some wanted to find and capture more horses, others to explore new territory.

Kol said, 'Dad, if you're going hunting, let me come with you.'

'Alright,' Knefrod said, 'but we go on foot. I'm only after hares today. Are you ready to go?'

Kol leapt off the bench where he'd been whittling a hazel-fork to make a catapult. 'Ready,' he said. 'Can we go and hunt in the earldom? I haven't been that way yet.' He pointed northwards. 'I don't know where to cross the river, but there's a forest in there—'

Knefrod spun round. 'No!' He held up a warning finger. 'Listen, all of you. We should have told you before. You must never go hunting across the river. You can ride there, you can walk there, you can run and play there, but never, never take your bows and arrows—never take any weapons, not even a catapult.'

'Is the Earl so selfish he wants to keep all the birds and wild game for himself?' Big Hengist asked.

'Nobody from outside the earldom is allowed to carry weapons in his land.'

'Why don't we raid them then, Dad?'

'Because we made a treaty with the Earl.'

Why?'

Knefrod sat down on the bench and looked round at the puzzled faces of the boys. 'Because we get tribute from him. We get tin, from the mines of Cornwall. The tin comes up in carts to the earldom and they bring it to us when we load our ships at the end of the summer.'

'But if we conquered the earldom we could keep all the tin.' Eric said.

Knefrod sighed. He wasn't a talking man. Hunter, seafarer, fighter, drinker, feaster, yes. Idol of women, he would say he was. But a talker, no. He wished some other dad would explain to the boys why the treaty and the tribute was good for the Vikings, but no other dad was there.

'If we conquered the earldom,' he said, 'the King of Cornwall would stop the tin coming. We'd have to go and conquer *his* land. And it's a drag of a distance from here. And then some of us would have to stay there to watch over the miners. But this way, well, it's easy. We take the tin and we don't attack the earldom. All you've gotta remember is, if you go there don't take weapons with you.'

'When did you make the treaty?' Horsa wanted to know. 'Go ask your dad,' Knefrod said. So Horsa did. The other boys, except Kol, followed him. Gus thought, 'Mordec would want to hear this.'

Harvald the Armourer said: 'When did we make the treaty? Five summers ago. We came in force to take the earldom. They guessed our intention. When we landed we found four of the Earl's men waiting for us, without arms. They told us that Earl Reginald wanted to parley and invited us to his castle. Twelve of us only, they said. So twelve of us went, and the rest waited on this side of the ford. We took our weapons with us. The Earl's soldiers ringed the battlements and lined the halls. He seated us at his table and ale was poured for us, and we feasted on roasted oxmeat. But we knew the guards were listening at the doors. And no women were in the hall. The truth was that the Earl half expected treachery, and so did we. We were careful not to drink too much. The Earl told us about the law against strangers bearing arms in his land. And what they do to anyone who disobeys the law.'

He paused and the boys moved closer. Titch's eyes were big with a mixture of excitement and fear. 'What do they do?'

'They try them in a court of law, and if they're found guilty they're condemned to death.'

'But how're they killed?'

'They're strangled with a cord and drowned in a black bog.'

Gus protested, 'Not warriors—they don't do that to warriors?'

'To everyone except knights. Knights are allowed to fight for their lives in the form of combat you saw on the Roman road.'

'But then warriors should be allowed to fight too.'

'Well, they're not. Anyway, the end of it all was that he told us he'd give us the tribute every year if we would never enter his land bearing arms. We were welcome as visitors, he said, but not as invaders. He said he'd had an understanding like that with Eyiolf the Bald, but Eyiolf wouldn't make a treaty. He asked us if we would. We said yes, and Olaf the Shipbuilder signed it for all of us because only he could write, and the Earl signed it, and that's the story. The treaty's been made, and don't any of you break it.'

the queen's story

Kol went hunting with his father. He liked creeping up on the quarry and hiding in the long grass almost as much as bringing an animal down with a well-aimed arrow. But that day he shot only one hare. His father shot twelve. They saw a hart in the distance, its branched horns like a wandering tree.

'I'll come for him another time,' Knefrod said. 'Now you go back. I'm taking the hares to a friend.'

Kol did as he was told. He found the village empty but for Hrolf and Bodvar who had been left on guard duty again and as usual were playing a game. He made for the river and was strolling along the bank when he saw Mordec fishing. At once, as if he had sighted prey, he dropped into the grass and kept watch.

Mordec had caught a rather grainy pike which would not be good to eat. He had seen more than one trout dart away and disappear, probably by lying perfectly still where the sunlight made its speckled back look like the pebbly river-bed. He cast his line five times before he caught one. He was not aware that two pairs of eyes were on him.

Lily was sitting in a tree within sight of the river-bank, and for some time she too had been watching him. She had seen someone else approach, stop, and crouch in the long grass. She could tell that he was another of the boy invaders, and his manner and movements told her that his thoughts were less friendly to Mordec than her own.

She hesitated, but soon made up her mind. She wouldn't let the croucher get away with his secret watching. She jumped down and ran towards Mordec shouting, 'Hullo.'

'Hush, please. You'll frighten the trout away.'

'Last time you didn't like it when I came up quietly, now you don't like it when I shout to let you know I'm coming.'

'For everything there's a time,' Mordec said. 'There's a time to be quiet and a time to shout. You get it the wrong way round.'

She sat beside him. 'I'll go away if you don't like me. But I *was* going to ask you to come home and meet my grandmother.'

'I'd like to. But not right now.'

'I also want to tell you that a boy's watching you.'

'A boy? What boy?'

'I'll tell you where he is, but don't look. Don't turn your head. I don't want him to know I've seen him.'

'Why not?'

'If we know he's there and he doesn't know we know, we're one up on him, aren't we?'

'What's he doing?'

'He's crouching in the grass and watching you. I think he doesn't like you.'

'Probably Kol. His father's a hunter,' Mordec said, not sounding bothered.

Lily was quiet for half a minute, then she said, 'Those small fishes over there taste best if you eat them alive and raw. I'll catch some for you now if you like. I do it with my hands.'

She stepped into the river.

'No, not now! Come back—you're chasing the trout away.'

Lily came back and sat down again, wet from her shoes to her knees. She asked abruptly, 'Are you an art director?'

'No,' Mordec laughed, which made Lily laugh too. 'What makes you ask that?'

'The only person I know who walks about with pieces of glass in front of his eyes is the Art Director at Linkard Castle.'

'I wear them because they bring distant things nearer. When I look at things close by, I take them off. And when I read if the letters are big.'

'You can read?'

'Yes.'

Mordec hauled in his line and cast it again. 'Now if she'll stay quiet—' he thought.

But no. 'What far-off things do you want to see?'

'I don't know yet. There must be lots to see. The world's big. The sea's wide.'

'You're funny. But I like you better than the other big yellow-head who thinks he can ride.'

'Gus? Gus can do most things better than the rest of us—running, swimming, wrestling, riding … I wish I could ride as well as he can. Or even better, as well as *you* can.'

'But you do things alone. Like fishing. And you laugh. But I think you need me to watch out for you.'

'*You* watch out for *me*? That's a laugh.'

'Yes, I will. I'm queen of this land and I promise I will. At least until the day when I can get rid of you all, dead or alive.'

'You won't put your dagger to my throat again?'

'No. Now come with me to meet my grandmother, Queen Bertha. That spying rat's still there but he won't bother us. I could scare that one sick, I know I could, and if he tries anything, I will.' She half lifted her dagger from her belt. 'Come on,' she ordered and started off, expecting Mordec to follow.

It seemed that fishing was over for the day. He picked up his meagre catch, tied the two dead fish together with string through their mouths, and followed Lily without looking round at the clump of long grass.

* * *

'There it is,' Lily said when they came within sight of a large weather-stained house set among meadows. 'Goosegarth.'

In the meadows horses grazed, Maelstrom among them. In the farmyard were geese and pigs. A few labourers moved about with buckets, pitchforks, and axes. There was nothing to surprise Mordec until he followed Lily into the house. He'd never seen anything like the long and lofty dining-hall with tapestries on the walls, a row of cushioned stools and chairs, and iron candlesticks like trees. It was three times as big as his father's mead hall. Plates and goblets were scattered over a wide oak table. The beams were grey with age, the floor was dusty stone, and some of the tapestries and cushions were slit and even ragged, but still there was a grandeur to the room, and the lady who came forward to greet him looked as Mordec imagined a queen should look.

Queen Bertha. Mordec could not tell her age; she was neither young nor old. Her face was brown, her hair black and shining, and her eyes had a sleepy yet laughing look. She wore a high-collared silk mantel edged with bear, which waved about her as she moved, her tread as soft as a cat's. She touched Mordec's hand with a forefinger and pointed with the same finger to a stool at the table, inviting him to sit down. He sat, carefully laying his fishing rod on the floor and his catch on a plate. Queen Bertha poured red wine into two battered silver goblets and set one before him. He sipped it tentatively. It tasted less sweet than the wine the village girls had brought, but it was heavier and had a strange perfume. He took a longer draft. Lily sat close beside him and watched him drink, and now and then she stroked his cheek.

'Eyeglasses are rare,' Queen Bertha said in languid, husky tones. 'Roman things. They make a man seem scholarly. Unusual for a Viking to be scholarly.'

'Yes,' Mordec agreed. 'In some ways I'm different from the others.'

'You're nicer,' Lily said, and stroked his hair.

'What other ways?' Queen Bertha inquired.

'I can read and write and the others can't. My mother taught me.'

'You're very young to be a warrior.'

Mordec opened his mouth to explain how it was that he had come on the summer voyage, but the queen went on: 'I've had friends among your countrymen. One I knew particularly well. We almost wed. Came very close to it. It was touch and go. He came in his armour and went in a shroud. Ah, he was a handsome man. The first time I saw him he boasted of his courage. I only laughed. "Osvald son of Olvir," I said, "it's a different kind of courage that a man needs with me." He gave me precious things, and I let him come again. And then he would not go away. The ships sailed without him. In those years they came in the winter, went home in the spring. Osvald son of Olvir stayed on, and late in the summer I buried his bones.'

'He died?' Mordec asked. 'Why? What happened?'

She gave him no answer. But she didn't seem sad that he was gone.

Mordec had never heard of this Osvald son of Olvir.

'So they,' Lily shouted, suddenly furious, 'the snakes, carried off my mother in revenge. I know it was all because of you, Gran, that they did it!'

'Who carried her off?' Mordec asked.

'Eyiolf the Bald. Because of *her*—' she pointed to her grandmother, 'I lost my mother.'

'Carried off?' Queen Bertha said. '*Ran* off, my darling, or to be precise *sailed* off in the ship of Eyiolf's son Ingolf.'

'You've made that up. She would never have gone without me if they hadn't made her.'

'You're a better girl, my dear, for being with me,' Queen Bertha said. She poured herself more wine and left the room with the goblet in one hand and in the other a short sword on which the raw liver and lights of a large animal were impaled.

'My mother is Queen Gloria,' Lily told Mordec. '*She* was the ruler of our country, not Grandmama. But Eyiolf slaughtered our army, and my mother was carried off, and our land was left undefended, and that's why you Vikings could come back and take it again with hardly a blow.' She glared angrily at Mordec, as though she hadn't been stroking him like a pet. 'One of these days you'll land here and find you've got to fight us again, or else turn and go back home.'

Mordec, not knowing what to say, cleared his throat and took another sip of wine.

Lily's tone became friendly again. 'I'm already the queen, really, but I'm not old enough to lead an army yet. When I do, the first one I'll fight will be Gus. Tell him that.'

'I will.'

'Now come with me, and I'll show you the Roman fort.'

She was out of the house and off down a winding path without waiting for him. He followed, leaving his fishing tackle and the fish behind.

among the ruins

'Come on, get up behind me,' Lily commanded.

'Will he let me ride him?'

'Yes, if I'm on him too.'

While Lily talked softly into Maelstrom's twitching ear, Mordec mounted. He put an arm about her waist and the horse started off at a slow walk.

Neither of them became aware that Kol was following them. He kept his distance but could hold them in sight because the land was mostly flat. The only trouble he had was finding anything to hide him, should they look round. He ran to a tree here, a thicket there, a dip in the ground, the slope of an old barrow-grave, the mud-wall of a pigsty or a border-wall of stones. He did it well, as he'd been taught. Kol the Hunter, Kol the Stalker, Kol who had plans and allies of his own.

The fort was a roofless ruin. Some of the outer brick walls remained. Maelstrom carried Lily and Mordec through an arch and they dismounted into the tall rough grass which had taken over the inner court. Leaving Maelstrom to await or follow them, they walked through broken halls. On some bits of wall cemented over with ancient lime, were traces of painted figures in pink and blue garments, a dim table and chairs, the outline of a crouching beast half concealed by a clump of real weeds which had found root-room in a gaping hole. A piece of floor was made of small flat black and white stones forming a picture of a bird's talons.

Several flights of steps led nowhere, but one, which they climbed, took them to a platform jutting out perilously from half-way up a broken wall. Lily sat on the edge of it, swinging her crossed legs, and Mordec stood beside her.

'We're waiting for Eyiolf the Bald to return,' she told him, 'and then we'll pay a ransom for my mother. Every year when you Vikings arrive my grandmother and I expect Eyiolf and his men to be among you, but they keep away. Listen, Mordec. Could you get word to Eyiolf? You say you can write. Tell him—gold for my mother.'

'You have gold?'

'Yes. It was his. But he'd plundered it from English courts and churches. We stole it back and hid it, and I think that's why he took my mother. That and revenge for Osvald son of Olvir.'

'And now you'll give it to him again if he brings your mother home?'

'Yes. Will you send word to him when you're back in your country?'

'I can't. I'm sorry. You see—' he sat down beside her to break the news, 'Eyiolf the Bald is dead. So are most of his men.'

Lily stopped swinging her legs and sat still. Mordec cast about for something he could say to comfort her.

'When I'm a bit older,' he said, not intending a promise, 'I could go and look for your mother.'

'You would do that?'

'Yes. I'd like to. Perhaps I'd take others with me. On horses. With arms.'

'Would you take *me* with you?'

He tried to think of something to say that would put her off.

'You'd have to find a ship to bring you to Trygghaven.'

'And shall I bring the gold?'

'If we find your mother, we'll get her back without paying for her,' he boasted. He imagined the scene now, a battle, victory, the rescue. But many years in the future.

'Then I can use the gold for something else,' Lily said.

'Like what?'

'To pay an army to fight the Vikings—to fight you, and free my land.'

Without thinking before he spoke Mordec said, 'Or you could just pay us to go away.'

She turned and stared at him, her dark eyes at his blue eyes, for a long minute.

'You would take gold to go away and never come back?'

'Well, *I* would.' Mordec said and laughed, but rather uncomfortably. 'I don't know if the men would. I can't make promises for them.'

'Ask them,' she said.

'How do I know there really is gold?'

'Do you think I'm lying?' Her eyes flashed angrily.

'No. I believe you.'

'I'll tell you where it is if you promise not to tell anybody except your Viking men, and only to tell them if they first promise to go away and leave us free when they've got it.'

'I give you my word.'

'I know you'll be true to it. Come. There's a place we can climb even higher.'

They descended, crossed more grassy courts, and climbed again, this time a longer, steeper, winding flight to the top of an old look-out tower. From there they could see far over the countryside.

'There's Goosegarth,' Lily said, pointing. 'And over there you can just see the turrets of Linkard Castle. Earl Reginald lives in it, and his daughter Jessica. It's full of things from far-off lands.'

'Books?' Mordec asked.

'Lots and lots. They keep them in a room they call a library. Jessica reads them. She'd teach me to read if I asked her to. She's my friend. Though really I should hate her.'

'Why?'

'Because her father made a treaty with our ene-mies—that's you.'

'Do you hate me?'

'As a Viking, of course. If I could free our land by killing you, I'd do it right now.'

'But aren't I your friend?'

'Yes, but sometimes a queen must kill a friend.'

the listener

Far below, Kol was hidden in a smelly, dark, timber lean-to, one of a row built in recent years against the lee wall of the ruin to shelter men and cattle from sudden storms and high winds. He'd heard Lily speaking of gold. It had made him catch his breath. But then they'd moved too far away for him to hear anything more.

'She's telling him where the gold is hidden and I can't hear a thing!' he fumed, peeping up at them from the shed.

When they started down the winding stairs he pulled back into the darkness of the shed. They passed quite near his hiding-place. He kept very still, waited until they'd moved on into the great courtyard where they'd left the horse, then crept along outside the wall until he was in line with them. He caught one word, though he couldn't be sure he'd heard it rightly. 'Addis,' he thought it was.

What did 'addis' mean, he wondered. Was it the word for something in this country that wasn't to be found in his own, or for something he knew by another name?

When Lily and Mordec had ridden away, Kol walked through the fort. Looking about him he nearly fell into a large square pit. He pulled back in time to save himself, then leant over cautiously to peer into it. Something was moving down there, and a moment later he saw what it was. Not one thing but many. He'd almost dropped in on a nest of vipers. The sight shocked him more than might be expected of a boy with a lust to fell dragons, and he fled.

white knight

On a path through a grove of birches, Lily and Mordec chanced to meet Sir Baz. The two horses, the black and the white, caught wind of each other and snorted before turns in the path brought them eye to eye. Sir Baz was in full armour but his visor was up. Courteously he turned off the path and waited for Lily and Mordec to pass by.

'Here is the knight who unseated Sir Cedric. Hullo, knight,' Lily said. And she added imperiously, 'Turn about and ride with us.'

Sir Baz bowed his head to return her greeting, and did as he was told. The horses walked on placidly, one behind the other through the grove, then side by side across the heath.

'I'm Queen Lily, the Viking behind me is Mordec, and my horse is Maelstrom. What's your horse's name?'

'Omar,' he told her in a mournful tone as though he much regretted it. But it wasn't the horse's name that caused Sir Baz to be mournful. Sir Baz was a gloomy knight. He told them that his life was lonely and hard. 'Yet,' he said, 'I suppose I am a lucky man.'

'How're you lucky?' Lily asked.

'Because I have a gift for combat. They say I'm the best fighter in England. King Louis of West Francia said when he knighted me that I was a better fighter than all his other knights. But he asked me to keep it quiet. He said they wouldn't like a man from another country to be better than they were. "You're not even a Frenchman", the King said.'

'What are you then?' Lily demanded.

'An Ethiope. And when I was a boy—about Mordec's age—I travelled and fought in Arabia, and there I won my milk-white steed in single combat with a full-grown man.'

'You are as black and beautiful and frightening as the night,' Lily said, who usually came straight out with whatever she thought, and did not sound in the least bit frightened.

'Why are you lonely, why has your life become so hard?' Mordec inquired.

'It's hard,' Sir Baz replied gloomily, 'to keep these white things clean when you're always moving on. They never have time to dry properly.'

'I'll take you home with me,' Lily said. 'My churls will do your washing for you. You can be my knight. I'm a queen, you see.'

'And you already have a hundred knights,' Mordec said.

'No,' Lily said. 'Not yet. But one day I'll have a hundred. Or a thousand. This one's the first.'

'And how can I serve you?' Sir Baz asked.

'I need to build an army,' Lily said, 'and I could start with you.'

'What do you need an army for?'

Lily tossed her head back to indicate Mordec. 'To get them, the Vikings, out of our land.'

'Are they cruel enemies? Monstrous tyrants?' Sir Baz asked. 'I haven't lived under them, you see—or not as far as I know. But then I haven't been in this part of England very long. Bad, are they?'

'He's not, he's lovely. He's clever. Sometimes I like him so much I could take a bite out of him,' and she bared her sharp little teeth. Mordec laughed and she joined in, but Sir Baz remained gloomy. He had nothing to say to this, and for a few moments they rode on in silence. Mordec would have liked to ask him more about his life in distant places, but before he'd got round to it Sir Baz, rather to Mordec's surprise, broke into a song. The words weren't jolly but the tune was, and Sir Baz sang it with zest.

I had a wife whose skin was white as Spanish alabaster.
They stood her up in London bridge to keep it ever after.
I had a dad who went to sea, a pirate on the water.
They hanged him from the yardee arm to dangle ever after.

Mordec thought that a man who'd known such violent loss should not be pestered to tell more. So instead of the questions that sprang to his mind, he asked the knight to sing again. Sir Baz, without looking the least bit happy about it, launched into the same song, and Mordec and Lily joined in.

When they'd dismounted at Goosegarth, Lily led Sir Baz into the grand and dusty dining-hall. No sooner did he set eyes on Queen Bertha, no sooner hear her voice greeting them, than he dropped clanking to his metal knees. 'Lady,' he said sorrowfully, 'may I forever be your knight. If ever lady was worthy of the courtly duty of a knight who would be fearless in her service, you are she.'

'Just a minute,' Lily said, standing in front of him and frowning, 'you're *my* knight, not hers.'

'Then let me serve this House,' he said. 'Two queens.'

'Alright then. But there'll be three, actually, when my mother comes home.'

'Yes, yes,' Queen Bertha said in her drawling, lazy way. 'I think I'd like to have a champion. Who are you?'

'Sir Baz, knighted by King Louis of West Francia. I am the Ethiope whom none would chronicle.'

'Whom none would chronicle? Will you drink wine with me?'

Sir Baz seized her hand and kissed it. He rose, took off various bits of armour and dropped them on the floor. Then he took the cup she poured for him, and drained it.

'And what are *you* searching for, young warrior?' Queen Bertha asked Mordec, who was looking under the table.

'The fishes I left here earlier,' he said.

'Fishes?' said the Queen. 'O yes, the fishes. I fed them to the little lioness.'

toast and treachery

In the Earldom of Linkard, not far from Linkard Castle, stood a small house built of dismal stone in which lived Mistress Codella Pillikin, also known as the Keeper of the Key, Coo to her friends. And in her house she accommodated a lodger, Master Bill Hitchem, also known as the People's Friend, for he was Duty Defender in the law court of the Earl. He was not very busy.

Cosy in the kitchen of the stone house, Master Hitchem was sipping an infusion of camomile and honey which Mistress Pillikin made every afternoon at five o'clock, and at the same time holding out a slice of bread on a fork towards the fire in the grate, when there came a knock at the door.

'Whoever could that be?' Coo wondered.

'You can only find out by going to see,' Bill said, not stirring from his task. The toast was coming along nicely. It was not the moment to interrupt its gentle browning.

'Well, well,' Coo said when she saw who it was. 'It's that boy,' she called over her shoulder.

'Which boy?'

'The Viking kid who talks through his nose. You know, the one with the topknot that we met in the forest?'

'Ah! Perhaps he brings news to share with us. Ask him to come in.'

'You can come in,' Coo said.

'Have some toast,' Bill said, pushing the slice he'd brought to perfection on to his own plate with a forceful thumb, and flinging the fork down.

Kol, knowing better than to take him up on this offer, came straight to the point.

'You asked me to find out if there was gold—'

'Yes, yes. Clever boy. You've found out, have you, and come to share the news with us? Well done! Out with it then—when and where?' Bill took up a knife and briskly spread butter on his toast.

'I know more or less where it is,' Kol said uneasily, 'but not exactly.'

'Not exactly?'

'Well, maybe even exactly, but you see—'

'Sit down, boy, and tell us all you know. Take your time. Are you sure you won't have some toast? Very well then, carry on.' Bill said encouragingly, and bit into his well-browned and buttered slice.

'I followed that boy I told you about. Mordec. He was with the girl they call Lily, the one who raced against Gus.'

'And?' Bill took another bite.

'They went to that big old ruined place—'

'You mean the Roman fort?' Bill asked, gesturing vaguely with the piece of toast in the direction of the fort.

'I s'pose so. And she told him—'

'Yes? What?'

'That she'd let him have this gold.'

'She said that?' Bill was suddenly so attentive now that he forgot to chew. 'Why? Did she say why?'

Kol didn't want to tell Bill why, so he went on, all in a rush. 'I came to say if you'll get the Wizard to change Mordec into something horrid and squirmy and low like—like a viper—I'll tell you where she said the gold is.'

Bill smiled his big smile, opened his mouth wide and took an enormous bite. 'C'mon, boy,' he mumbled with his mouth full, so that bits of buttered toast flew out of it. He gulped some of the mouthful down and went on chewing rapidly. You can share this with me. Of course we'll get the Wizard to change Mordec into whatever you wish. Aren't we here in this world to help each other?'

'Are we? Oh. Good. Well, then he asked where is it? And she said—'

Yes? C'mon on, out with it boy!'

'I—I *think* she said that it was in something called …'

'Called what, boy? Don't whine. Speak up.'

'Something called an *addis*. I don't know what it is but I thought maybe you'd know.'

Bill stopped chewing and held his toast aloft, perfectly still, as he thought hard.

'An addis?'

'Yes. That's what she said. Would you please tell me what it is?'

'Well now. The thing is—er—which addis? Did she say *which* addis?'

'No. Not that I heard.'

Bill popped the last piece of toast into his mouth. 'Well boy, that's very useful, very interesting, but it's not quite enough. Thing is, you didn't listen properly. Not enough to go on, you see. Go back and find out what this Mordec fellow talks about. Watch what he does. Watch and listen, listen and watch. We'll help each other, won't we? *I'll* have a talk to the Wizard, and *you'll* find out exactly which addis they're talking about.'

'I think it would help if you told me what it is.'

'I can't do that. Not unless I know more. There's more than one type of addis, you see? Off you go now, and come back with more news as soon as you can. Oh—and if you want me to get the Wizard to change Mordec into something, it would be best if you could get him to me, here in the earldom. D'you understand? Run along, no time to waste.'

'But—'

'Sorry you won't stay longer and have some more toast with us, but we quite understand. Good-bye,' Bill said.

Kol still hesitated. Coo gripped his elbow and hustled him out.

'Come again soon,' he heard Bill's voice calling hospitably before she shut the door.

southward bound

Walking back to the village without his trout and feeling quite hungry, Mordec thought about two things, food and Lily's offer. He made a plan or two. 'It'll have to be leeks and pancakes without meat or fish tonight. And I'll tell Olaf the Shipbuilder or Harvald the Armourer about the gold. They might consider it a good exchange, gold for freedom. I would.'

But nothing turned out as he expected. He found that Isolde, the plump woman who wore Knefrod's silver armband, had jugged some hares and was spooning out the thick stew for all the boys. Big Hengist was on his third plateful when Mordec joined them, and he had three helpings too.

Later when he went to Big Olaf's house, he found him asleep, sitting up in a comer of the bench with his head bent back and his mouth open, snoring loudly. So Mordec went quietly away and knocked on Harvald's door but got no answer. 'I'll tell them about the gold tomorrow,' he resolved.

In the morning he found that the men were preparing for a voyage, hurriedly loading two of the ships. Big Olaf was on the landing-stage, giving orders.

'Where are we going?'

'South,' Big Olaf said. 'A short voyage. But you boys will stay here.'

'I've got something important to tell you.'

'Not now. When I'm back.'

Most of the men were going. 'We're off to pillage, plunder, and trade,' a slow-moving carter named Svein bragged to the boys.

'No, only to trade,' Big Olaf said.

'What will you bring back, Dad?' his son asked.

'We've heard of a glut of wool coming to market. Good English wool and it'll be cheap. At Yaremouth wic. Only two days' sailing to the south. We always get a good exchange, furs for wool.'

'The word is they're selling slaves there too,' Hakon shouted.

'We shouldn't buy slaves now,' Gunnar the Sailmaker advised. 'Our slave market's too far east or south. We'd have to trade them on to Halfdan's land-crossers, and meanwhile we'd have to feed them and find space for them in the ships.'

'They could row for us,' Svein said, who liked finding ways to save himself hard labour.

'Not worth it,' the Sailmaker said, 'at the prices Halfdan pays.'

Knefrod wasn't going. He'd be in charge of the village, with Hrolf, Egil and a few others to guard the boys and the livestock and things. But at the last moment the boys were told that seven of them could come too, 'to carry the wool bales to the ships'. They shouted with glee at the news. But which of them would stay behind? Big Hengist said he would because he'd asked Isolde to give him cookery lessons and he was impatient to begin. Then Mordec said he would too because although he'd have liked to sail south and see the town and the market, he wanted to visit Linkard Castle and its library. And then, rather to everyone's surprise, Kol mumbled that he'd also stay. He didn't say why.

a trap is set

Kol had his doubts about Bill. Would he keep his side of their bargain? If not, Kol thought as he made his way to his father's house, some other way must be found to deal with Mordec.

He looked round the door to see if Knefrod was alone. He was.

'Dad? I've got something to tell you.'

'Make it quick. I'm going after that hart we saw. And this time I'm going alone.'

'You know that girl called Lily who won the race? Well, she says she knows where gold is hidden.'

'She told you?'

'N-no. She told someone else, but I heard her.'

'When was this?'

'Yesterday.'

'And did you see a dragon too?'

'Dad, I'm telling you the truth this time.'

'Don't you always?'

'Well—anyway. I'm not absolutely certain where this gold is, but I'm going to find out. And when I do, we can go and get it. Just you and me. I know someone else who's after it, but you can easily frighten him off. He wouldn't even fight, I'm sure of that. In fact, he'll lead us to it, and then we can grab it.'

'Alright. I'll tell you what to do. You trail this easily frightened person, and when he finds the gold, give me a shout.'

'You don't believe me, do you Dad?'

'I'll believe you when I see it. Just make sure I do see it.' Knefrod set off for the forest. Kol strolled thoughtfully back to the boys' house and nearly bumped into Mordec who was coming out with something in his hand he was taking bites of.

'What's that you're eating?' Kol asked.

'Isolde calls it a sausage-roll. She and Big Hengist are baking them. Try one.' And he walked off towards the river with a look of having something important to do.

'Where are you going?' Kol called after him.

Mordec didn't answer. Kol watched him go, thought of following him again, but turned instead into the house. Two full-cheeked pink faces were bent over rows of pastries steaming on a baking-tray.

'Here, try one of these,' Big Hengist said. 'I made them.'

'Careful of your fingers—they're still hot,' Isolde said.

'Where's Mordec going?' Kol asked, blowing on one of the rolls and snorting as he took a bite.

'To the earldom,' Big Hengist said, lifting the sausage-rolls one by one on the wide blade of a knife and arranging them on a large platter.

'Now, Hengy,' Isolde said, 'let's go back to your dad's place and I'll show you how to spit-roast the suckling-pig.'

Left alone, Kol chewed thoughtfully. He took another bite of his sausage-roll without really tasting it, then suddenly dropped the rest of the thing on the floor and ran to the end of the bench where Mordec usually slept. There on the wall was Mordec's big bag, and beside it his sword. The sword went into the bag. A bow and a quiver of arrows followed it. Kol looked about for more weapons, but decided against taking things that belonged to the other boys. Then he remembered an axe which one of the English labourers had left behind when they'd come to fix the roof. He'd kept it for himself and had hung it in his father's house. He went to get it. Isolde and Big Hengist were so busy basting the suckling pig they hardly glanced up when he came in, and said nothing as he left with the axe in his hand.

Carrying the bag he hurried after Mordec and soon saw him up ahead, following the line of the river. Keeping his distance he watched Mordec crossing the ford into the earldom, and waited awhile, watching carts being driven through the shallow water and folk on foot picking their way across on the stepping-stones. When Mordec was out of sight, he crossed over, looking about him furtively. Was anyone eyeing the bag, wondering what was in it? Not that he could see. Afraid but determined, he struck off down an empty lane in the direction of a certain small stone house, choosing paths through copses and long grass, hoping to meet nobody on the way. He did though, as he rounded a bend in a narrow path through an ash grove, and for a moment he froze with fear. But he recovered quickly when he saw that the person coming towards him was the very man he was looking for.

'Ha! So it's you, my young friend,' Bill said, smiling his large smile. 'And I see you've brought something to share with me?'

Kol stepped off the path and in among the trees and beckoned to Bill to follow him. When they were close together and well hidden, Kol opened the bag and Bill looked at what was in it. He gazed thoughtfully at the sword, the bow and arrows, and the axe, then up at the treetops, keeping the smile fixed on his face. At last he whispered to Kol who nodded and whispered back. Bill took the bag and went off with it towards the castle, and Kol turned and hurried back the way he'd come.

He ran across the river, splashing through the water rather than dilly-dallying over the stepping-stones. Only then he slackened his pace and strolled along the bank whistling, feeling unusually light-hearted and looking forward to a dinner of suckling pig.

the wizard

When Mordec came to Linkard Castle he found that the drawbridge was down and the portcullis up. There was no moat, only a paved space in front of the entrance which was flanked by watchtowers. All round the rest of the castle the green turf grew to the base of the walls.

Mordec walked right into the castle precincts without anybody stopping him. Then he looked for someone to speak to and at that moment heard a voice calling, 'Whoo-hoo, whoo-hoo!' from an open window. He looked up and saw Mel, the Art Director, waving. He waved back. 'Come in, come up,' Mel called, and pointed to an open doorway.

Mordec entered the castle. The light was dim but he could see a flight of wide stairs and he made for them and climbed to the first landing. There Mel was waiting for him.

'Now don't tell me,' he said, 'it's … Mordec! Am I right?'

'Yes,' Mordec said.

'Delighted to see you Mordec,' Mel said, and really sounded delighted. 'Come this way. I'd like to show you my studio.'

Mel led him into a big bright room. Silks, flowers, ribbon, embroideries and tapestries were heaped on trestle tables. 'Fol-de-rols and thing-a-lings,' Mordec remembered.

'I'm in charge of Ceremony, Decoration and the Wardrobe,' Mel said. These are the materials I work with. Did you come to consult me?'

'Yes. I came to ask if I—'

'I'm delighted to hear it. The good Earl doesn't mind a bit that I go in for a little private practice on the side. Moonlighting, as it's called. If my reputation has spread far and wide it's because I have a good track record. So clients keep on coming.'

'A track record?' Mordec repeated. 'What exactly is it you do for your—clients?'

'For them, to them. I change them. I make them over. I wave a magic wand over them and turn them from frogs into princes, or princesses. May I ask, is it a total new image that you're after, or simply to look your best for a special occasion? The main question in your case is—can you see well enough if you leave the glasses off? In my own case the answer is no.'

'I used to take them off to read,' Mordec said. 'I still can, but it's getting harder. And speaking of reading I was wondering if I could—'

'I trained at a court in the south of France,' Mel went on, 'though my special tutor was a Spaniard. And I do have a natural talent. Truth to tell, I'm an absolute wiz at it. In fact, they call me The Wizard, you know. Ask anyone.'

'I believe you,' Mordec assured him.

'The first thing I have to persuade you to believe is that *outsides matter.* Of course they're not everything. There's more to making the right impression than simply looking good. In public life it's essential to have a certain aura. Call it charm.'

'And isn't it also good to *know*—?' Mordec said, more to make a point than ask a question.

'Oh I always assume that my clients *know*. Know more or less where they want to get to, anyway. My job is to help them get there. And as I was telling you, the dear Earl, bless his heart, doesn't mind a bit. Goodness knows the job I have here gives limited scope for my talents. I can design the liveries, I can set the scene for special occasions, and there are a few gentlemen of the court who like to look their best. But on the whole the Earl has chosen rather—shall we say, *dry* men. Men of law, and a sober cleric. Any old thing will do for them, they say, as long as it's clean, mended and paid for. The ladies of course are better customers. But Lady Jessica does not set an example of encouraging a sense of fashion. For herself, of course, she doesn't need it. In the simplest thing she looks ravishing. To put anything ornate on her would be to hide her beauty. It would be like painting the lily or putting gold leaf on pure gold. Linen, wool or silk—she looks a dream in all of them—Who's there?'

He took a step towards the open door, peered out, and listened for a moment. 'Funny—I thought I saw someone. I thought it was one of my former clients. But I must have been wrong. Perhaps you've met him? Master Bill Hitchem, the court Defender. They call him the People's Friend now, and it's true that a lot of people find him perfectly delightful. But it wasn't always the case. Not to put too fine a point on it, he used to be an absolute dragon. He owes his new character entirely to me—though he had to put in a lot of work himself. Smiling came hard to him. I made him practice in front of a looking-glass for hours and hours. And if I say so myself, he's one of my greatest successes … That you Bill? Funny—I thought I saw him again. But no. Nobody's there. I would have called him in to bear out what I say.'

'I don't think I'm old enough to need a new character yet,' Mordec said.

'Ah. Perhaps not. So there's nothing I can do for you then?'

'Well, yes please, if you would. I'd very much like to see—to see round the castle. Do you think—'

'Certainly, dear boy, certainly I'll show you round. Come along.'

linkard castle

Mordec thought Lily and Bertha's house grand, but the castle far grander. As he moved from hall to hall, from chamber to chamber, up and down wide stairs and narrow stairs, his eyes roved over displays of shields and weaponry on the walls, and tapestries, and painted scenes. On landings statues stood, and complete sets of empty armour, at which Mordec peered to see how the joints were made, especially in the inside of the elbows and the backs of the knees. It was all very fine, he thought, and daily life was much more comfortable here than at home. Men in livery stood at doors looking very superior with their faces turned up, and others scurried along passages with their faces down. And some, it seemed, crept about spying on others. More than once Mordec thought he saw a figure in green and red nipping out of sight just as they rounded a comer.

'Now I wonder,' Mel said, 'would you care to see the library?'

'Oh, yes please. I would. I'd like that very much.'

'This way then. It's a fine room, what you can see of it. Unfortunately, much of it is hidden by the books. Books, books, books. They're all in cages, too. Anyone would think they could bite.' He laughed.

'Shelves and shelves of them, right up to the ceiling.'

'Do you read them?'

'I? No, I could but I don't. Sometimes look at their covers when others have them down. I just love the interlaced curlicues of gold, and the tiny birds and beasts. Some, you know, are inlaid with ivory, and some have their spines edged with embroidery in silk threads of many colours.'

'But you don't read what's inside them?'

'Bless you, no. I'm far to busy to read. Only lawyers and clerics actually open the books. And a few ladies. This way. In here—'

'Halt!'

Two guards clad in chain-mail and helmets had been standing still as ornaments, one on either side of the entrance to the narrow passage leading to the library, and it was one of these who spoke now. He stepped in front of Mordec, barring his way.

'Who are you? What's your business here?' he asked Mordec sharply.

'I can vouch for him officer,' Mel said. 'He's my guest. One of the Vikings, you know, who visit every summer.'

'A Viking, eh?' The guard stepped back and snapped an order at the other guard. 'Search him.'

The one who gave the order had a red feather on his helmet, the other a blue. Their visors were raised and Mordec could see that they were not much older than himself. Blue-feather leant his pike against the wall and clapped Mordec's arms and legs, chest and back.

'What is it you're looking for?' Mordec asked.

Neither Red-feather nor Blue-feather answered the question.

'Weapons,' Mel whispered rather loudly. 'It's illegal for visitors to carry them.'

'I'm not carrying any weapons,' Mordec said.

Blue-feather clapped the tops of his boots and said, 'He's clean.'

'Clean?' Mordec said, and laughed. 'Of course I'm clean. My mother raised me this way. Hands always washed before cooking and eating, and a bath three times a week.'

'In what?' Mel asked as they strolled on past the guards, who had again taken up their positions on either side the tunnel-like entrance to the library.

'In what?' Mordec repeated, puzzled by the question. 'Water. Brine. Melted snow. Whatever's available.'

'Hot or cold?'

'We warm the water in winter.'

'And do you put herbs in it?'

'No, I put herbs in food.'

'Try rosemary in your bath. Or roses. Or crushed chestnut—that's my favourite. But it's hard to come by. The trees grow in Byzantium. By the way—' Mel paused with his hands on the library doors, turned his head and nodded towards the guards. 'How do you like the uniforms?'

'Oh yes,' Mordec said, not knowing what else to say.

'Not entirely my design. The smith adapted them. Couldn't myself see why it was necessary but he claimed there were technical reasons. The single feather was my idea. Start with blue, rise to red. The captains have yellow. Now—here we are.' He pushed open the pair of thick oak doors and closed them carefully again when they'd both passed through.

'Odds-bods!' Mordec said, catching his breath. He had not supposed that there could be so many books in one place. He went to the nearest bookcase and peered at the leather backs of the lower volumes to read the titles. *Sermons. Sermons. Sermons.*

'What,' he asked Mel, 'are sermons?'

'Long speeches made by priests. Too long, usually.'

'I know what you mean,' Mordec said feelingly. 'Ah, there's one called *A Geography.* D'you think I could take it down and open it?'

'We'll ask Father Donlock—he's the librarian. A churchman,' Mel replied in an undertone.

'Churchman?'

'Of course, I forget. You folk have not embraced the Christian faith. I admire you for sticking to your own ways. It's a matter of taste, as I see it, like everything else. But you have priests, don't you? Well, the librarian is a kind of priest. Learned. Sober. Serious. Very, very dry. Wears the same thing day in, day out.'

Just then the doors opened and a tall lean man came in. He was dressed in black. His cheeks were sunken, his nose long and narrow, his grey hair cut short. 'Father Donlock,' Mel said softly to Mordec.

'Father, my young friend Mordec would like to see inside a book.'

Father Donlock stared with narrowed eyes at the young Viking. 'But you can't read, can you?' he asked.

'Yes, I can. My mother taught me.'

'Runes or Roman letters?'

'Both.'

Father Donlock's eyebrows arched with surprise.

'And what sort of book do you want to see?'

'A book with maps of the lands and charts of the seas? Or are there any that tell about the stars and planets? And what lightning is? And why some mountains shoot out fire?'

The priest turned to close the doors, and Mordec saw that the crown of his head was a bald circle wreathed by grey hair.

'Yes, there are. And about birds and beasts. Are you interested in birds and beasts?'

'If they're real.'

'Some are only known because travellers tell about them. They may or may not be real.' And still the man studied Mordec's face and made no move to show him books of the kind they were talking about.

'The Geography over there—' Mordec said.

'Ah, that was given by Ceolfrith to King Aldfrith, and it was used by the Venerable Bede.'

'Where do they come from, all these books?' Mordec asked. 'Who wrote them?'

'Many minds and hands composed them. Some were brought here by the Earl's grandfather, who went to study in Italy.'

'Was he a churchman?'

Father Donlock smiled thinly. 'No. Nothing like a churchman. Though he was something of a scholar.'

'Which did he bring from Italy?'

'You are specially interested in Italy? Why? What do you know of it?'

'Nothing much. But my grandfather lives there.'

'Ah-hah!' Father Donlock said, closing his eyes for a moment, as though to seal into his head this particular piece of information, the first that had come from Mordec which seemed to make sense to him. 'Well,' he went on, and tapped one of the cages, but made no move to open it. 'That Homer, for instance, written on paper, and these homilies in folio, on vellum, and do you see the octavos over here, well they were all carried over land and sea by Bishop Theodore of Tarsus and are part of a small surviving remnant, saved by a brave subdeacon from the great library at Canterbury which Theodore founded, and which grew to be the most important in England. All gone, all gone—but for these few volumes. Think of it, that whole vast treasure of thought, record, scholarship, all gone, all lost.' He shook his head and Mordec thought he could see tears in his eyes.

'How did it get lost?'

Father Donlock bent a little towards Mordec, though the boy was almost of his own height. He looked through Mordec's glasses and watched his blue eyes widen as he told the terrible truth: 'Like all the other libraries in England it was destroyed by your people, my lad. They wantonly put them to the torch.'

'Odds-bods! Whyever did they do that?'

'You are in a better position to tell me than I to tell you,' Father Donlock said drily. 'A small part of the great collections was saved and kept in private hands—safe, we hope from invaders. A treaty the Earl made with you Vikings was partly to protect this heritage.'

Mordec was sure now that Father Donlock would not take down a book for him to look at. 'He doesn't trust me,' Mordec thought with shame.

'Come, dear boy,' Mel said, 'There's more to see.'

Father Donlock nodded at them both and glided away.

'I don't envy his job,' Mel said as they went down the narrow passage and passed between Red-feather and Blue-feather. 'As well as the Earl himself, who is not exactly a book-loving man like his grandfather but likes a bit of a read now and then, there are all the others, the lawyers and clerks and pages, as I told you, and even some of the ladies who *will* keep getting books down from the shelves. You can't keep a shelf looking right when people do that sort of thing all the time.'

***

A few minutes after Mel and Mordec had left the library, the double doors were opened again, little more than a crack, and Master Bill Hitchem put his head between them. Father Donlock frowned when he saw who his visitor was this time. But he asked politely, 'What can I do for you, Master Hitchem?'

Bill smiled, opened the doors a little wider, and brought the rest of himself into the room. He stuck his thumbs into his belt and swept a casual glance over the spines of the books.

'Father,' he said, 'I'm not as lucky as you.'

'I beg your pardon,' Father Donlock said, 'I don't know what you mean.'

'I mean I haven't been molded by education. I can read and write, I'm not an entirely ignorant man, but—'

'I'm sure you aren't,' Father Donlock said. 'If you know right from wrong, that's enough to be getting on with. Do you know right from wrong, Master Hitchem?'

'That, and a little more,' Bill said. 'But there are certain streams of knowledge to which my floodgates were never opened.'

'Never opened,' Father Donlock repeated, 'I'm sorry,' he added, in case sympathy was wanted.

'Latin,' Bill said.

'Ah,' Father Donlock said.

'Now into you, Father, Latin poured like a river in spate. Am I right?'

'I studied it.'

'Then you can share a little of that learning with me, if you would. Help me, if you will, to solve a simple little mystery. As you know, my place in court is simply to tell the prisoner's story. The judges may sometimes talk in Latin, but it's not expected of me.'

'So I understand.'

'But sometimes a phrase—a word—drops on me. And I feel that it would refresh me to know its meaning, even if I may never drink deep.'

'Is there a word or a phrase you would like me to translate for you?'

Bill stopped and turned to look at Father Donlock with an expression of acute admiration.

'There now! What it is to be a man of education! How quick your understanding is, Father. Yes, a word. One word. If you please. If you could tell me its meaning.'

'Certainly. What is it?'

'Addis.'

'Addis?'

'Just so. Sounds Latin to me. Is it?'

Father Donlock didn't say no or shake his head, so Bill pressed on.

'I gathered—from the way it was used—that it means some part of a building—am I right?'

'Some part of a building? Not that I know of. The only meaning I could put to it is—'

'Yes?'

'Well, now. It's the second person singular, present tense, indicative, active, of—'

'Yes?'

'Of addo, addere, meaning—'

'Yes?'

'To add.'

'To add.'

'Addo, addere, addidi, additum. So addis means "you add".'

'*You add?* You are sure of that, Father?'

'Yes.'

Bill placed a forefinger on each of his closed eye-lids and pondered. Then he looked brightly at Father Donlock again. 'Or could it perhaps mean a part of a building which has been added? Now that would make sense, wouldn't it?'

'It could mean *you build on,* but not *something* built on. If there is such a word for a part of a building,' Father Donlock said, 'I don't know it.'

'But there could be?'

'I suppose there could be.'

'Fine. Fine. That's what I needed to learn. If we can learn one new thing every day. Father, we will never tire of life. Thank you.'

Father Donlock nodded. Bill went out and closed the doors. And Father Donlock soon gave up trying to understand why someone should ask a question and yet disdain the answer.

* * *

'Now what else may I show you?' Mel asked.

'How about the kitchen?' Mordec suggested.

'Ah, yes, the kitchen. One of these days they'll let me loose on the kitchen. A whole new field for me. Down this way. I'll leave you there and get back to work. Come and see me again, please do.'

The kitchen was wide and deep and high. It was well-stocked and full of bustle and good smells. Mel left him with a girl named Peggy who was in charge of a churn. She asked him his name and where he came

124

from, and then pointed out objects of interest. The spit didn't need a hand to keep it turning but worked on a system of wheels and weights and ratchets, like Horsa's grandfather's straw dolls. The deep ovens in the wall of the enormous fireplace could bake twenty loaves at a time. The hams on the hooks in the chimney were smoked by an ever-burning fire. Standing before the fireplace whose chimney breast was as high as he could reach, Mordec could almost have believed that he'd wandered into a land of giants; yet the people, most of them, were quite small.

'The fire,' Peggy said, 'blazes day and night. Every day it burns a whole oak tree. We've a fireman keeps it going. There he is, that's him. Ally-pally,' she called to a man dozing in a comer. He opened one eye. He was of brown complexion with a broken and rusty helmet on his head, and leather clothes so stiff and hard and scorched that he looked like a creature who'd been forged in a smithy rather than born in a bed-chamber. 'This is Mordec. He's a Viking. Mordec, this is the fireman and his name is really Alexander Syria, but we call him Ally-pally.'

Ally-pally rose slowly, creaking a little, to a height more Viking-like than English.

'Ally-pally, dear, please take my friend to see the cellars and the woodstore.'

The iron man lit a torch and Mordec followed him down sooty steps into a dungeon. 'See?' said Ally-pally, pointing. 'The oaks is brought by the woodmen ready chopped up an' they drops 'em down from that 'ole above, and 'ere they lies for me t'get at. Now over 'ere we keeps the wine an' ale, 'undreds and 'undreds of jugs an' jars an' butts an' bottles.'

Footsteps coming down the stairs and a ringing command made them turn.

'Halt!'

Red-feather appeared, Blue-feather behind him, and Mel last of all.

'Show him the bag!' Red-feather ordered. Blue-feather advanced and held out for Mordec's inspection a blue leather bag that was astonishingly like his own. 'But it can't be mine,' he thought, unable to see the thing very clearly in the flickering torchlight. 'Anyway, there must be lots of old blue leather bags in the world all looking the same.'

'Open it!' Red-feather commanded.

Blue-feather dumped it on the sooty ground and Mordec opened it.

'Odds-bods!' he said when he saw what was in it. Then he remembered that weapons were what they had been searching for. He looked up at Mel.

Mel shook his head to show he was as mystified as Mordec. 'They found it in my studio,' he said. 'I've no idea how it got there. Someone must have put it there, but I told them it wasn't you. I distinctly remember that you weren't carrying anything when you arrived. But as you're the only stranger they've seen here this afternoon they insisted that I show them where you are.'

'Is this your bag?' Red-feather asked sharply.

'I don't know. It looks like mine. Can we take it into the daylight?'

Mordec began to lift it but it was snatched from his hands by Blue-feather who then moved round behind him. 'Follow!' Red-feather commanded, and led the way. Mordec went next, then Blue-feather, then Mel, and last came Ally-pally. As they passed through the kitchen Peggy stopped churning and watched with her mouth open.

Through the kitchen door they went into a herb garden bathed in the rosy light of late afternoon.

'Now then. Is that your bag?' Red-feather asked again. Mordec knelt to look at it, and stared again at what it contained. He reached for the sword.

'Leave it!' Red-feather barked. 'Show it to him!' Blue-feather took out the short sword which old Harvald had made and held it out for Mordec to examine.

'Yes,' Mordec said. 'That's mine. And the bag's mine. But I didn't bring them here.'

'And these?'

Out came the bow and the quiver of arrows.

'They could be mine. I'm not sure.'

'And this?'

Mordec looked at the axe. The end of its handle was bound with tin.

'No,' he said. 'I've never seen that before.'

'That's a good one! The bag's yours, the sword's yours, but this you've never seen before.'

'That's right. And I've no idea how the bag and the sword got here.'

Red-feather stepped forward.

'What is your name?'

'Mordec son of Hauk.'

'Right then. Mordec son of Hauk, I arrest you for violatin' the law of this land, namely that no stranger may carry weapons while within the borders of the earldom. I have to tell you that you will be given a fair trial. Until you are summoned to the court you'll stay locked up in the Tower of Doom. Bind his hands.'

Blue-feather took out a length of cord and tied Mordec's hands behind his back.

'This is most unfortunate,' Mel said. 'I shall go and speak to the Earl myself and tell him that I saw you arrive—and that you were empty-handed—'

'No more talking to the prisoner,' Red-feather said. 'March him to the tower, and I'll get word to the Keeper of the Key.'

tower of doom

The tower was not far from the castle. It was built of the same grey and dismal stone as the house of its Keeper, Mistress Codella Pillikin.

'Pillikin's my name,' she said to Mordec as she unlocked the iron door with the iron key which hung on one of the leather straps that kept her wrapped up like a parcel. 'But because of my sweet nature, folk call me Coo.'

With a guard in front of him and a guard behind him, Mordec ascended a winding stair, up and up and round and round, until they reached a little landing at the top and there another door was opened by the Keeper of the Key. The guards stood aside and Mordec followed Coo into a room with a floor unevenly coated with mottled white bird-droppings. On the ledge of the window a raven sat now, looking in resentfully at the intruders. He flew off cawing, spreading the news to other ravens, and when his noise faded Mordec could hear a thin wind whistling round the tower. A small heap of broken straw and a torn blanket lay in one corner, beside a chipped earthenware plate and jug crusted with hardened gunge.

'Stale bread and dusty water you'll get,' Coo told him, pursing her lips between phrases as though for a kiss. 'And be thankful for that. Remember there are boys of blameless character in Nimmerlinesland who'd be glad to have bread and water brought to them without it costing them a penny. And look what else you've got, you lucky lad! Come here to the window. What a view, eh? See how the ground shines over there as though it's all wet and sticky? Well, it is. That's the Bog of Brockalee, and you'll be seeing more of it before long. Hoo-hoo-hoo!'

Chortling, she went out and locked the door behind her. Mordec went to the window and looked down. The ground was a long way off. If he jumped he'd break his bones. And he could see two guards posted at the lower door, one with a red feather on his helmet and one with a blue. Mordec could tell that they were not the same pair who'd brought him here.

He wondered if anyone at home in the Viking village would miss him and come looking for him. Perhaps Mel would send word so they'd know what had happened. If Olaf the Shipbuilder and Harvald the Armourer had not gone away they could have been depended on to sort out this confusion. All he'd done was come to see the castle and the library. He'd committed no crime. But how had his bag come to be in Mel's studio, and who had put his sword in it? If someone did it to get him arrested and imprisoned, who could that someone be? Surely no one hated him that much, not even Kol! And Kol didn't know the law of this land—or did he?

An hour or more must have passed during which Mordec felt his spirits sinking as steadily as the sun, when he heard voices, then footsteps on the stairs and the unlocking of the room door. In came Ally-pally with a covered basket.

'If it was up to me,' Coo's voice came from the landing, 'I wouldn't allow this. It's only spoiling him. What's he done to deserve special treatment, I'd like to know.'

Ally-pally winked at Mordec and set the basket down on the floor beside the bed of straw. 'Peggy packed it,' he said. 'She went to Lady Jessica, y'see, and Lady Jessica's 'eard all about heverythin' what's 'appened from the gen'leman yer was with, an' she tol' Peggy t'send a proper dinner. There it is now. I'll bid yer g'night. Yer c'n look f'me agin in the mornin'.'

In the basket Mordec found hard-boiled eggs, fresh white rolls, butter and honey, a thick slice of ox tongue, a ripe plum, and a jug of fresh cold water. The meal made him feel better in more ways than one. He was not to be forgotten and abandoned.

He sat leaning against the stone wall with no light but the moon which printed the shape of the window on the floor, and after a long time he fell asleep.

* * *

Ally-pally came again in the morning as he'd said he would, and with him another visitor.

Father Donlock waited while the iron man replaced last night's basket, and when he'd gone stood looking down at Mordec.

'The Earl,' he said, 'is the fairest judge in all England. There was a time when bad men came to the Earldom of Linkard to commit their crimes because they knew that if they were caught here they'd get a fair trial and they wouldn't be tortured. The Earl, the one we have now, did away with torture, you see. And he did away with trial by ordeal. Here prisoners do not have to hold burning brands so that the judges can find them innocent if their wounds heal and guilty if they don't. Oh yes, they do that in other parts. But the Earl set up trials rather like the Romans used to have. One man accuses the arrested person and brings witnesses to back up what he says. Another man defends the arrested person and brings witnesses to back up what *he* says. The Earl and the other judges decide what to believe. The side with the most witnesses has the advantage, of course. If the accused person is found guilty, he's punished. Do you understand everything I've told you so far?'

'Yes.'

'Well, at first the punishments were not as severe as they were in other parts. But when the Earl found out that villains came here to do bad things just because they believed that nothing very bad would happen to them, he made a change. He made the punishments much more frightening.'

Mordec was listening to every word.

'When the news spread,' Father Donlock said, 'that punishments here were as bad here as anywhere else, bad men kept away. Now, do you know what the punishment is for a serious crime, like the one you are accused of?'

Mordec shook his head.

'I'll tell you. For serious crimes such as stealing hogs or bringing weapons into the earldom, it's death. What happens is this. The condemned person is strangled first and then pressed down into the Bog of Brockalee. Ever since that punishment came in, nearly ten years ago, it's only been carried out three times. There's very little crime in the earldom. Now I didn't come to tell you this just to frighten you. I think you should know the facts.'

'But I haven't done anything wrong,' Mordec said, staying calm and reasonable though it cost him some effort.

'You are accused of one of the worst crimes. And in your case bringing weapons into the country not only breaks the law but also violates and endangers the Treaty of Linkard which was concluded between the Earldom of Linkard and the Vikings five years ago.'

'But I didn't know. I didn't know about the treaty. And I didn't bring the weapons. I only came to see the castle and the library.'

Father Donlock looked at him thoughtfully. 'I'll be back,' he said.

When he had gone Mordec wished he'd asked him for a book. Then he thought, 'But he'd never lend me one. Not after what we did to books in England.'

He turned his attention to Ally-pally's fresh basket, and was soon breakfasting on apple and curds, brown bread and ale.

No sooner had the last crumb gone down with a good wash of ale than his door was unlocked again and this time in came a stranger dressed all in red and green. The head was put in first, smiling, then the rest of him followed. Mordec remembered seeing this person on the day of the jousting and the horse-racing.

'I,' said the newcomer, perching himself on the window-ledge, 'am known as the People's Friend. And with good reason. I defend the underdog against the rich and powerful. I shall defend you at your trial. I've come to hear your side of the story so we can convince them they've got the wrong man. Right?'

'O yes, right!' Mordec said, keen to encourage this kind of help as much as he could.

'My name,' the smiling man went on, 'is Bill Hitchem. Please call me Bill.'

'Bill,' Mordec said, happy to please.

'Now they say you brought a bag of weapons into this country. Is that so?'

'Yes. I mean no. I mean, they say I did, but I didn't. Mel, the Art Director—he saw me arriving and he'll tell you I wasn't carrying the bag. I wasn't carrying anything.'

'He may say that, but—'

'Don't you believe him?'

'*Of course* I believe him. But who's to say you hadn't brought it earlier and put it in his room *before* he saw you?'

'But I didn't. If they say that, won't they have to prove that I—'

'Well, I'll just have to make the best I can of *your* account of what happened,' Bill said, rising. He turned to look out of the window. 'Wonderful view you have here,' he said, yawning and stretching. 'But the weather has been rather dry, wouldn't you say? In very dry summers it's been known for the mud level of the Bog of Brockalee to sink so low that the heads of the drowned have stuck up all over the place like rotting stones. Then the rooks and ravens come and peck out the dead men's eyes.'

Mordec swallowed hard.

Bill began to pace about the room. 'When it comes to trials and evidence and arguments, nobody can be certain of what will happen. Unfortunately, innocent men are condemned, guilty men go free. It happens often. Despite one's noblest efforts.'

Mordec swallowed again.

'There's one way though that is not so …' he rocked a hand from side to side, 'so icey-dicey. I am speaking of the use of money. You understand what I mean?'

'No.'

'When the resources are in place, then one can be sure. I think I have made myself perfectly clear, haven't I?'

'I don't quite see—' Mordec began to say.

Bill waved away all doubts and objections.

'Such resources would not of course be for my services. I am paid by the earldom, not well, and yet well enough to allow me to give away much of what I earn to the poor. But there are too many who are disadvantaged. Deprived. Are you with me?'

'No.'

'To come straight to the point,' Bill said, stopping his pacing, sticking his thumbs under his belt and looking down with a frank and friendly expression at Mordec, 'do you have any money?'

'No.'

'Nothing that would pass for money? Like—gold, perhaps?'

'No.'

'Not *on* you, of course. I don't mean in your pocket,' and Bill laughed so heartily that Mordec felt he should laugh too, but no sooner did he show willing by starting to smile than Bill's face became sad and grave.

'Ah, that's bad. Sad. Bad and sad. Here I am, struggling to find a way to save you, and you're not helping me. Perhaps you fail to understand just how serious your situation is. Think now—do any of your Viking friends know where gold might be obtained? Hmmm?'

'I don't know.'

'Where are they, these Viking friends of yours?'

'Most of them sailed south.'

'And when will they be back?'

'In seven days. Maybe.'

'Seven days. Maybe. They may be back just in time for the trial. On the other hand, they may not. It would be better if you could think of a way to direct me to a little gold. The means to a better life for many a poor family.'

'I can't. But I didn't do anything wrong.'

'What about your English friends? The noble Queen Bertha, or her dear little granddaughter? Do they have any gold?'

'If they do,' Mordec said, 'I don't think they'll give it to you to save me.'

'Ah!' Bill said, shooting a forefinger out to point at Mordec. 'So you don't deny they have these gold resources?'

Mordec rose. 'At the trial,' he said, 'I'll tell the judges that I didn't bring that bag with the weapons into this country. They'll have to believe me because it's true. And if they won't listen to me, you must tell them.'

'Of course I'll do that. Trust me. And meanwhile, think about what I've said. If you want to get a message to me at any time just tell Mistress Pillikin, she'll know where to find me. Good-bye for now. No need to thank.'

When his duty-defender was gone, Mordec felt more uneasy than he had before. He went to the window and watched the ravens flying about the tower, listened to the wind whistle round it, saw the ominous gleam of the Bog of Brockalee, and wished he knew who had plotted against him, and why.

treasure hunt

A trudge beyond the Tower of Doom and a huff and puff beyond the Pillikin house, stood yet another structure built of the crusty grey stone. In the lintel over the iron gate, which was locked by the same key as the door of the tower, its name was carved: Bond House. A gravelly yard surrounded it, fenced with iron, and darkened rather than shaded in one comer by an ancient and dispirited yew tree. Within these narrow precincts were strictly housed and sparsely nourished the bondsmen who laboured for farmers, tradesmen and craftsmen, to work off debts their families owed and could not pay. Some were in bond for a few years only, others for longer than they could hope to live. Clad uniformly in grey, they worked every day from sun-up to sun-down except on Sundays, when they had to go to church in the morning, but in theory were left to their own devices for the rest of the day. From this Sunday-afternoon desert of time, Master Bill Hitchem, a man with a calling to cure unhappiness, worked out many a plan to redeem them.

Not for long did they have to languish on the prickly needles fallen from the yew tree on hot summer Sundays, or rack their wasted brains over a game of

Little Soldiers with gravel-stones on a 'board' marked in the dust. Nor on winter days huddle for too weary a while round a very small fire of chips and pine-cones smoldering in the very small grate in a comer of the icy hall where, on benches at trestle-tables twice daily, they swallowed their gruel and broke their hard grey bread with their teeth, or their teeth with the hard grey bread. Winter or summer, these fleeting hours of leisure would barely have begun when, more often than not, they'd be cheered by the voice of Master Hitchem, hallooing from the iron gate or the iron door: 'Good news, good news! I have wangled permission from the Keeper of the Key to take you all on an outing!'

In the firm belief that human beings are happiest when they are doing good to one another, Bill Hitchem liked to pitch his fellow mortals, bond or free, into public works. 'Fun, fun, fun,' he would cry to hearten them, and even regale them at his own expense with healthy drinks made of gagwort and dandelion. 'No need to thank. And please call me Bill,' he'd say, to bond or free, for he believed that all should be equal as well as unselfish.

On the first Sunday after Mordec the Viking had been arrested and locked in the Tower of Doom, good Bill Hitchem, the People's Friend, appeared at the iron gate of Bond House just as the thirty inmates, old and young, were letting their weary bones sag in the sun-warmed dust. His rallying cry rang through the compound: 'Hulloo! Hulloo! Fun, fun, fun! You'll never guess what we're doing this afternoon! Anybody want to try a guess?'

Nobody did.

'Then I'll tell you. It's something really special. A *treasure huntl* What do you say to that?'

Nobody said anything.

'Don't say your friend Bill doesn't think about you and bring colour and joy into your lives.'

Nobody did.

'Up then, and off we go! Chickens and Ladders in front.' The bondsmen were never called by their given names but were known instead by the work they were most often put to or the things they used when they worked.

Coo, standing smiling beside Bill, unlocked the gate, and the bondsmen, young and old, knowing that they had no choice, arose blear-eyed from the needly shadow of the yew tree, left dusty games unfinished, and took their places in a long grey line behind Chickens and Ladders. Coo held the gate open and Bill came striding in front to lead them out and onward. 'Step out lively now, m'lads,' Bill called. He tilted his head back and snuffed the breeze. 'Ah!' he said, 'fresh air and exercise—nothing like it to make you glad to be alive!'

He took them over empty fields. No one was about. Sunday afternoon was the people's nap-time. No one to see them, no one to hear them.

'Sing!' Bill commanded. 'Let's sing our marching song!'

He lustily, and the rest drearily, sang:
We march towards the rising sun.

The singing, though scarcely more than a moan, made the grey line all the more breathless.

At the door of Mistress Pillikin's house, Bill stopped. Near it, picks and spades lay in a heap. At the sight of them the grey line's spirit gave in and its parts sank to the ground with groans. Up, up, my friends!' Bill exhorted it. 'We haven't yet begun!' Slowly it rose. Bill put tools into its hands. 'Aren't you excited?' he asked it, with his bright smile and bright eyes. He himself shouldered a coil of rope. 'On, on!'

Tools on shoulders, heads down, the grey line trailed after him again. 'Sing!' And it sang. It mattered not to it which way it was led so it failed to notice that it was nearing the narrow stream politely named the River Witter, the border between Linkard and the East Fenreach, which bondsmen and bondswomen were forbidden under threat of direst punishment to cross. Only when Bill stopped where the three stepping-stones began did the line look up, and then it squirmed and murmured.

'Special permission to cross today, signed and sealed by the Court,' Bill said. He pulled a roll of vellum from his belt, and waved it about. It had a big read seal on it, and a wide red ribbon dangling from it, so it looked very official and correct.

No voice of the line asked to read it. No head in the line could read.

'To comply with the conditions laid down *herein*,' Bill went on shaking the roll at them but not opening it, 'and much as it grieves me, I must rope you together.'

This he did. Rope went round the middle of each body and on to the next until the line was strung together like clothes pegs on a market stall.

'On!' Bill said.

Over the ford it went, the many-footed line, fear on its faces. Rumour had it that Bondsmen had been sunk in the black Bog of Brockalee for doing nothing worse than this.

'Sing!'

Again the line sang as it marched on to the Roman fort. Among the ruined walls it stopped and Bill addressed it.

'You will understand why you have been permitted to come on this outing, and you will be as glad, as heart-warmed as I myself, to know that the treasure we shall dig up this afternoon is to be given to the poor.'

The grey line did not leap for joy, but Bill was not surprised. He understood the hearts of his fellow men. If they were not so hard he would have no need to dedicate his life to softening and sweetening them.

'This way!' He led the line to the side of the ruins where the wooden sheds leant against the old brick wall. This, he guessed, must be the 'addis', the part *added on*. 'A clear mind,' he'd said to Coo, 'can light its own way, even without education.'

'Line, halt!' he ordered. 'Now hear this. We don't expect to find the treasure with the first dig. It will take time and patience, but we will stick at it. It's an ongoing process. Right? Right. Start here. Picks first, then spades. And good luck, men!'

The grey line sighed and got to work.

hot pursuit

Mordec had been in the tower three days and nights. He could do nothing to help himself until his trial. He wondered if there was anybody 'out there' who might try to do something for him—some investigating, some talking to the authorities. Gus, he thought, would do something if he could think what to do, and if he'd been near. But Gus had sailed away with the men. Of those still at the village, Egil and Hrolf would do what they were told to do by Knefrod, and Knefrod wouldn't tell them to help Mordec. Not if Kol had any say in the matter. Then there was Big Hengist. Not a bad guy at all, but not a man of action and not a great brain either. So much for his own folk. What of the people of the earldom? There was Bill, the People's Friend, who might or might not defend him successfully at the trial. There was Mel de Gustybuss who would certainly speak for him. And there was Lady Jessica, who wished him well, but could do nothing to prove his innocence.

But there was someone he didn't think of. The last person anyone would expect to come to the rescue of a Viking. Lily. She was doing all she could.

In the very hour of Mordec's arrest, a farmhand named Walter had crossed the Witter, as he usually did on these fine long evenings, and made his way to a back door of the castle to meet his lady-love in the herb garden when the light was rosy and the scents were sweet.

'Walter dear,' Peggy said after the first cuddle, for she was his lady-love, 'Walter, one of them Viking lads was taken up by the guard this afternoon and they've stuck him in the Tower of Doom. They say he was plotting to attack us all in our beds, but I don't believe it. He seemed a nice lad.'

'A Viking?' Walter said. 'I was told they'd sailed off south most of them and weren't to be looked for again in a week or more.'

'This one didn't sail. He's in the tower for sure.'

'I've seen one or two of them lads. The one that raced against our Queen Lily, and the one that wears glasses.'

'That's the one.'

'Our Queen Lily won't like it if that one's in trouble. I saw her hugging him, making a real fuss over him. Viking or no Viking, she's taken to him.'

'Tell her what's happened then,' Peggy said. 'Our Lady Jessica doesn't like him being in the tower, but there's precious little she can do about it, the Earl being such a stickler for the law and all. It's my belief that someone set him up. And Lady Jessica thinks so. And Ally-pally too, and I've never known *him* be wrong. The poor lad's all alone. Perhaps your Queen Lily can get word to the Viking dads wherever they've got themselves to. So you tell her.'

'I will,' Walter said. He and she had a few more cuddles, and when Peggy had to go and help with the washing-up, Walter made his way back to Goosegarth where he was pigman, and there soon told his tale.

Sir Baz was the one who heard it from him. The mournful knight liked to come down to the sty and watch the pigs at the trough. He promised to pass on the news, and when he went to down a goblet or two with Queen Bertha, he told her what he'd heard from Walter. It wasn't long then before Lily heard it too. Without a word to the others she slipped out, fetched Maelstrom from his meadow, and on his back reached the castle before the sun had sunk into the Bog of Brockalee. When she'd heard all she needed to know, first from Mel and then from Jessica, she rode through the twilight to the Viking village.

From Egil she found out which coastal market it was that the Vikings were bound for to trade their furs for wool. 'The wic at the mouth of the Yare,' he said.

'How many days sailing?' she asked.

'With the winds fair,' Egil said, looking up from the arrows he was feathering by firelight and turning his head seaward as though he could watch the winds blowing, 'two, three at most. Is it Gus you want? More racing, is it? He'll be back in a week or little more.'

'They must all come, all of them, to save Mordec,' she said. 'He's been locked up in a tower for taking weapons into the earldom, and they'll put him on trial for his life.'

Egil said he already knew about it.

And it was true that he did. The Earl had sent a courier to inform the Vikings. They had listened and drawn aside to confer among themselves. Was the Earl about to attack them on the grounds that one of them had broken the treaty? Now, while so few of them were here? No, no, if that was the Earl's intention he wouldn't have sent a courier, would he? And in any case, wouldn't he fear Viking revenge? They'd returned to the courier and told him, smiling, that they saw no reason to get hot and bothered about young Mordec getting himself into a spot of trouble. The Earl was known to be a fair man who ruled by law. The courier had taken the answer back to the Earl, and the faces of the Vikings had lost their smiles as they watched him go. They recognized the danger in what had happened. And now the young Queen of the Fenreach was meddling in it.

'You mean to ask them to break the treaty?' Egil said. 'No chance. They'll never do it. If Mordec broke the rules he'll have to face the punishment. They won't make war for him.'

'Do you know what the punishment is?' Lily gasped, amazed at the lack of fire in this man.

'No. Yes. Let me think. Taking weapons into the earldom? Odds-bods—it's death!' He looked a little more concerned but not what Lily would have expected of a warrior hearing of a threat to one of his band. 'But he'll be tried first. If he didn't do it they'll let him go.'

'And if they don't believe he didn't do it? If they won't let him go?'

'We still wouldn't invade the earldom.'

'Are you the one who says so? Do the others do what you say?'

'Well, no, not exactly. But they wouldn't—you can believe me.'

Lily was exasperated. With her hands on her hips and head bent she strode about for a minute or two, frowning as she thought of another plan.

'Maybe they will for gold.' she said at last.

'For gold?'

'I know where gold is hidden. I told Mordec to tell them. I wanted to give it to you—to all of you—to go away and never come back. But now I'll give it to you if you'll save Mordec.'

Egil tried to picture himself alone saving Mordec, and Lily rewarding him with the gold. He'd become a hero and rich at one stroke; but he knew that even with Hrolf and the others who'd been left behind to guard the village, they couldn't win against the strength of the Earl's regiment of guards.

'If the gold is such a heap that it's worth breaking the treaty for,' he said, 'we'd need more men, ten times as many—no, a hundred times as many to make war on the Earl. It would take weeks to send a ship home and bring back enough fighting men. But you can tell me where the gold is, and when they get back …'

Lily didn't stay to hear more. She mounted Maelstrom. Big Hengist came out of doors, yawning, in time to see her go. 'What was that all about?' he asked.

'That Queen Lily. Looking for Gus and them,' Egil mumbled.

Lily urged Maelstrom into a gallop and heard only the wind—the enemy wind, warm and light and steady, blowing southward, sending the men who could help Mordec steadily further and further away.

She found Sir Baz in the barn at Goosegarth, glumly grooming Omar. 'How long', she demanded, 'would it take to ride to Yaremouth'?

'If I rode night and day.' he replied, 'taking the Roman road, and not wearing my armour, and resting the horse only just enough, I could do it in a day, a night, and half a day.'

'Tell Grandmama that's where I've gone, to fetch help for Mordec. D'you hear me? You must do exactly what I say. And tell her if I'm not back with *them* in time to save Mordec she must make the Earl let him go.'

'Make the Earl let him go?' Sir Baz shook his head sorrowfully. 'The Earl's a stickler for the law. Even your grandmamma, who could persuade heaven to abolish winter if she wanted to, couldn't talk him out of that. He has a noble heart but a governor's head.'

'Then she must drug him. Tell her to drug everyone in the castle except Jessica if I'm not back with the witnesses in time. And then she and you must snatch Mordec out of that tower. Tell her that.'

'Drug them? And snatch Mordec? I could laugh at that, if I could laugh,' Sir Baz confessed to Omar—not to Lily, because she was gone.

* * *

She rode hard, though not as fast as Maelstrom might have carried her because she had Roman Ruin on a lead-rope. She'd fetched him from the field beside the Viking village, slipping past the guards again.

It was the length of time she kept the horses going rather than the pace that made the beasts sweat. She let them rest and graze at the roadside every now and then because she knew she must, but not for long—except on the second night when she slept for four hours instead of the two she'd allowed herself.

For the rougher travellers on the road she took care to seem a poor and shabby boy so they wouldn't think robbing her was worth the trouble. The few coins she had were sewn into the hem of her tunic, and her dagger and a short sword which had once belonged to Osvald son of Olvir was concealed in the back of her belt under a short stiff mantel such as pigherds wore in the rain, and which did in fact belong to Walter the pigman. But the value of her horses she could not disguise, and she half expected to be set upon for the prize of her blue-black stallion or the fine and tamer bay. What she did not know was that the sight of a boy pounding along the road on a powerful steed and drawing another beast behind him at an urgent pace made villains step aside, thinking this must be a reckless horse-thief with an avenging squadron hot-hoof on his trail.

the trial

'Hall right then, wakey-wake. Day of yer trile. Got yer breakfiss 'ere. M'lady gave horders as ya was to 'ave roas' lamb—t' keep yer strength up. An' Peggy 'as sent yer a pitcher of hale—t' keep yer pecker up.'

Mordec only took in half of what Ally-pally said to him, but he needed no reminder that this was the day of his trial.

'Good luck to ya, boy!' Ally-pally said, briefly putting a heavy hand on Mordec's shoulder.

Mordec did what justice he could to the lamb and the ale, though he had little appetite and thought the lamb could have done with a rosemary garnish, and that the ale had a smack of mouse in it. He washed himself as best he could with the small jugful of water and the tiddly little basin which Mistress Pillikin, his jailer, had assured him was 'no smaller than the Earl himself has in his chamber'. So this was how Englishmen washed, at best! Though English ladies were friendlier to water. 'Lady Jessica, now,' Mistress Pillikin had said, rather bitterly, yet shaking her head as though more in sorrow than in anger, 'has Roman baths, one hot one cool, big enough to swim in, summer and winter.' And then she'd heaved a sigh and added, 'While there are wretches in Nimmerlinesland who never see a drop of water from one year's end to the next!' Mordec had wanted to ask where this dreadful Nimmerlinesland was so that he might avoid it, but before he could utter another word the Keeper of the Key had stamped out and locked the door.

He put on his clothes and his glasses and believed he was as ready as he could be to face whatever the day might bring.

'Here they come now,' he thought, as footsteps sounded on the stairs, 'to take me to court.'

The door opened, and in walked Mel, dressed in his working smock, followed by two pages hefting a painted box between them which they set down on the floor.

'Well, hello!' Mel called cheerily. 'A very good morning to you, dear boy.'

'I didn't expect visitors this morning,' Mordec said. He waved the back of a hand over the remains of his breakfast. 'Will you have some breakfast? The baked lamb's not bad, and the ale has an unusual taste.'

'Thank you, no,' Mel said. 'I've had mine and we must get on. I'm your witness, you know? I'm going to tell them you were not carrying that bag when you came to the castle.'

'Thank you. Then will they let me go?'

'Well, the other side has a witness too, unfortunately. And to win you have to have at least one more witness than they can produce.'

Who's their witness?'

'I'm afraid I've no idea. But that's not what I've come about. I've brought you your costume.'

'My costume?'

'O yes, I designed it specially for you. I always do the costumes.'

'For trials?'

'For every public occasion. I'm given a pretty free hand. The only limits on my imagination are the limits of my stock. I buy fabrics madly whenever the merchants come from France, but I can't anticipate every need. This time—bit of luck. English cloth. Look. Tell me frankly what you think.'

He opened the lid of the painted box and took out a garment of coarse-woven grey wool, patched in many places with squares of linen and leather.

'Try it on,' Mel said. 'You can only judge a garment properly when it's on. When you see the hang and the movement.'

'Do I have to wear a special costume to be tried?'

'Well, it's not part of the law. It's for the drama. And don't you see the effect this will have? You must admit—its heart-rending. Here—let's get it on you.'

Helped by the pages, Mel stripped Mordec of his tunic, leggings and shoes and put the sad garment over his head. It hung droopingly from his shoulders, as if his strong frame were thin and frail.

Mel turned him this way and that. 'Nothing too hor-rifying, you see. I resisted the obvious temptation to add bloodstains, or streaks that could be read as a brought-up breakfast. Poor but clean and mended—that was the look I wanted. A garment not kept in luxury, but not maltreat-ed either. Penitent if found guilty, humble if acquitted. A thing that speaks for itself sorrowfully and sincerely.'

But though Mordec felt it might seem unkind to reject Mel's creation he said firmly, 'No. Thanks, but no.'

Mel looked wistful. 'Are you sure? Don't you think it might—?'

Mordec shook his head and put his own things on again.

Mel considered. 'Maybe if you just took your shoes off before you went into court. I do advise it. I truly believe that if you keep them on—good strong shoes like that—they will make the court think you are rather—strong, and—that you know what you are doing.'

'Well I *am* strong. And I usually *do* know what I'm doing. Though it seems I can be tricked a bit too easily! But—alright, alright,' he said hastily as he saw Mel opening his mouth to try more persuasion. 'I hear what you say, and if I remember to, I will. But I do have rather a load on my mind.'

'I can understand that. It's the uncertainty, isn't it? Well, it'll all be over by lunch-time, one way or the other, and then you can relax.'

Mordec opened his mouth to comment, but Mistress Pillikin's voice arrested their attention, calling in a loud and formal tone from half-way down the stairs: '*Prisoner! You are summoned to the court!*'

'Off you go, dear boy. Best of luck,' Mel said warmly. 'See you in court.'

Mordec descended. A platoon of armed red-feather guards awaited him outside the tower, rank on rank, four abreast.

He was taken aback by such a show of strength. But he said as calmly as he could, 'I'm glad you realize how dangerous I am.'

One of them seized his shoulder and pushed him forward until he stood in the midst of them. Off they marched, the clanking contingent and their boy prisoner who held his chin up and his shoulders back and took long strides.

The portcullis was up, the drawbridge down. As soon as they were inside the walls, the drawbridge was raised and the portcullis dropped. Two of the guards detached themselves and Mordec from the platoon. Between them he crossed the courtyard, passed through an archway, continued down a vaulted passage, and entered a vast hall through a pair of iron-studded doors which were shut behind them with two resounding thuds. He saw a wide table at one end, a number of men in dark robes and flat hats seated round it, the Earl in the middle, his hat and gown edged with wolf's fur. Half way down the length of the hall, on either side, was a carved chair. On one sat Bill, the People's Friend, hugging himself, his wide-smiling bright-eyed face aglow with cheerfulness. On the other drooped a black-robed, grave-looking old man, bent with age. His hair and beard were long, thin, and grey. A roll of parchment in his hand was trembling like a wind-tormented leaf.

Mordec was left standing in the middle of the floor. He planted his feet apart, pulled himself up to his full height, and squared his shoulders. Not one Viking could he see among the spectators. There were a few English faces that he knew. Mistress Pillikin was among the crowd, and in a small gallery sat Lady Jessica and Father Donlock. Lady Jessica smiled at him, and he smiled back.

'Prosecutor, read the charge,' the Earl ordered gently.

The old man rose slowly to his feet, unrolled his scroll, silently read something in it and rolled it up again. 'Prisoner,' he began, in a quavering voice, 'are you the Viking known as Mordec son of Hauk?'

'Yes.'

'You are charged that in deliberate defiance of the laws of this land and in flagrant disregard of the historic Treaty of Linkard concluded between the Earldom of Linkard and the Vikings, you, of your own free will, without instructions from any authority, made an armed incursion into our sovereign territory. How do you plead, guilty or not guilty?' Mordec started and shook his head, dislodging his glasses from the top of his nose.

'An armed incursion? Odds-bods!'

'Answer please—guilty or not guilty.'

'Not guilty.' He settled his glasses back in place.

'Bring in the senior arresting guard.'

A door beyond the judges' table opened and the red-feather guard Mordec had seen first near the library on that fatal afternoon came and stood stiffly facing the judges.

'You found the bagful of arms, you and your blue?'

'Yessir.'

'Tell the court where you found it.'

'In the studio of the Art Director.'

'You then confronted the prisoner with it?'

'Yessir.'

'You showed him the bag and he said it was his?'

'At first he said he wasn't sure but when he'd looked at it in the daylight he said it was his.'

'And did he say the weapons inside it were his?'

'One of them, sir.'

'So then you arrested him and ordered his imprisonment?'

'Yessir.'

'No more questions.'

The Prosecutor returned to his chair.

'Has the Defense any questions?'

Bill Hitchem rose to his feet and asked: 'I understand you had searched the prisoner earlier that afternoon?'

'Yessir.'

'And you'd found no weapons on him?'

'None sir.'

'Would you tell the court why you later went to the studio of Master de Gustybuss and searched for the bag which you found?'

'A note was found sir.'

Bill clapped his hands. 'The note, please.' A blue-feather guard brought it to him. It was a piece of curling tree-bark in which a few words had been scratched. Bill read them to the court: *Viking weapons in bag under table of M de* G.' Is this the note that was brought to you?'

'Yessir.'

Bill handed it back to the blue-feather guard who took it to the judges' table.

Bill went on with his questions.

'Who found the note?'

'I did sir.'

'Where?'

'On the floor near the lie berry sir.'

'So you've no idea who wrote it or dropped it there?'

'No sir.'

'Very good. Ve-ry good. I have no more questions.'

The guard was dismissed. The Prosecutor rose again. 'Bring in Kol son of Knefrod.'

'Kol. Of course! I should have known,' Mordec said to himself.

Kol came in. He avoided meeting Mordec's eye.

'Come and stand where the judges can see you,' the Prosecutor ordered, pointing with a shaky forefinger to the spot where the guard had stood. 'Now I want you to answer my questions truthfully, do you understand?'

'Yes.'

'You have come forward of your own free will to give evidence in this case?'

'Yes.'

'Even though the prisoner is a fellow Viking?'

'Yes.'

Why is that?'

Kol's jaw hung slackly open. He looked up at the beams as if they might tell him what to reply.

The Prosecutor prompted him. 'Could it be because you love truth more than loyalty?'

'That's right.'

'Well, well. The court is no doubt pleased to hear it. Now, tell me, have you seen this bag before?'

The Prosecutor beckoned to a red-feather guard who stepped forward and held up Mordec's bag.

'Yes.'

'Louder, please, and look towards the judges as you answer.'

'Yes, I've seen it before.'

'When did you last see it?'

'When I carried it for him—'

'For the prisoner?'

'Yes.'

'When was that?'

'When he told me he was coming to visit the castle, about a week ago.'

'Did he ask you to carry it?'

'Yes.'

'Is he the sort who likes to give orders?'

'Yes.'

'And are you the sort who likes to obey them?'

'N-no, but—I don't mind doing a favour for a friend.'

'Good friends, are you?'

'Yes.'

'Did you carry it for him all the way to the castle?'

'No.'

'Where were you when he took it from you?'

'At the ford.'

'At about what time was that?'

'I don't know, but it was before noon.'

'Did you cross the river at the ford and come with him into the earldom?'

'No.'

'Did you know what was in the bag?'

'No.'

'What did you think was in it?'

Kol shrugged. 'No idea. His fishing things, maybe.'

'You didn't ask him what was in it?'

'No.'

'To the best of your knowledge, did he pack the bag himself?'

'Yes.'

'Now just a minute, Kol!' Mordec called out, unable to restrain himself any longer. 'You know that what you're saying is—'

'Silence, please,' the Earl said in a kindly tone. 'The prisoner will speak only when he is spoken to. Guard, show the weapons.'

The guard stepped forward again and laid out a row of weapons on the stone floor: Mordec's sword, a bow, a bundle of arrows, and an axe with a tin-bound handle.

'Prisoner,' the Earl asked, 'are these yours?'

'The sword is mine. The bow might be. The axe isn't. But what I want to tell you is—'

'That's all for the moment, thank you. Prosecutor?'

The Prosecutor went on: 'Now tell me, Kol son of Knefrod, do you know that a treaty has been made by the Vikings with this earldom by which the Vikings have promised never to attack, never to make an armed incursion, and always when visiting this land to obey the law which forbids every visitor to bear arms while he is within its borders?'

'Yes.'

'Who told you?'

'My father, Knefrod son of Kol.'

'And did he tell only you, when the two of you were alone together, or did he tell all you boys at the same time?'

'He told us when we were all together at the same time.'

'And was this before Mordec son of Hauk entered the earldom?'

'Yes.'

'How long before?'

'The day before.'

'And are you quite sure that Mordec son of Hauk was there when your father told all of you about the treaty and the law?'

'Yes. We were all there.'

Mordec clenched his fists with fury. 'You're lying Kol—I wasn't—'

'Prisoner at the bar, will you be silent?' the Earl asked, more as though he were offering him something nice to eat than rebuking him for speaking out of turn.

'Thank you, I have no more questions.' the Prosecutor said. He returned to his chair.

'And the Defense?' said the Earl.

Thinking that his chance to speak had come at last, Mordec began, 'Yes, I do have some questions—'

'Quiet, please. One more outburst and I will have to banish you from the court,' the Earl told him, still

without the least trace of anger. 'The Defense, please.
Master Hitchem?'

Bill Hitchem rose and turned his smile on the
judges. Perhaps now they'll hear the truth, Mordec
hoped. There was a long pause. 'No questions,' Bill
said, and sat down.

Mordec could hardly believe his ears. His defender
had turned down the chance to cast doubt on what
Kol had just said. Kol was to get away with his lies!
As Kol left the hall, Mordec stared at the Earl and
the judges, hoping, even expecting that someone at
the table would now ask him for his version of what
had happened. But none of them was looking at him.
No one seemed the least bit interested in anything
he might have to say.

He twisted his head round to look up at the gallery.
Lady Jessica had her eyes fixed on him intently. She
nodded, one little nod. He felt it was a sign of en-
couragement, but what exactly did it mean? Perhaps
that his turn to speak was yet to come. But when?

'Now, Master Hitchem,' the Earl said, 'call your
first witness.'

'I call Master Mel de Gustybuss.'

Mel came in through the door behind the judges
and stood in Kol's place. He was dressed in a long
purple robe belted with silver. It made him look rich
and important. Master Hitchem took a few paces
towards him and turned to the judges. On them he
kept his eyes as he put his questions.

'Did you see Mordec son of Hauk arriving at the
castle on the afternoon the bag of weapons was found?'

'Yes.'

'At about what time was that? Soon after noon?'

'Not soon after, no. Maybe an hour or so after.'

'And was he carrying anything in his hands when he arrived?'

'No.'

'You're quite sure?'

'Quite sure.'

'No more questions.' Bill returned to his chair.

'And the Prosecution?'

The Prosecutor rose.

'You say you saw the prisoner enter the castle precincts?'

'Yes. I happened to be at my first-floor window which overlooks the main yard and I saw him come through the big gate and stand there looking about him. I had met him before on the day of the joust, so I waved and called, and when he waved back I invited him in.'

'And he had nothing in his hands?'

'Nothing.'

'He brought nothing into your room?'

'Nothing.'

'Then what happened?'

'We chatted for a bit and then I offered to show him round the castle.'

'Why did you do that?'

'He asked me to.'

'Ah-hah. You say he asked you to?'

'Yes.'

'Did he ask you to present him to the Earl himself?'

'No.'

'Did it occur to you that he might have had it in mind to do harm to the Earl?'

'Good heavens no, why should he?'

'Master de Gustybuss, I ask the questions, you give the answers. Was there anything in which he seemed particularly interested?'

'Yes. The library.'

'The library? Did it not strike you as odd that a Viking should be interested in a library?'

'No.'

'Then what happened?'

'On the way to the library the guards stopped and searched him.'

'Did they find anything?'

'No.'

'He had no weapons on him?'

'No.'

'Did he then enter the library?'

Yes.'

'And once there, what did he do and say?'

'He asked me whether he could look at some of the books.'

'And that did not strike you as strange?'

'No.'

'What did you say?'

'I said he could ask the librarian, Father Donlock.'

'And did he?'

'Yes. Father Donlock came in and they talked about books. He said he could read both Roman letters and runes.'

'The Viking prisoner said that?'

'Yes.'

'And you believed him?' the Prosecutor asked, smiling briefly at the judges.

'Yes.'

'Then what happened? Can you remember?'

'I remember Father Donlock telling him that certain books in our library had once been in the great library at Canterbury and were saved when it was burned, and he—the prisoner—asked who had burned it, and Father Donlock said that his people, the prisoner's people, had done it. He said they'd burned all the libraries in England.'

'Ah. The Vikings had burned all the libraries in England. Yes. We know that to be a fact, do we not?'

'I do now.'

'And how did the prisoner react when he was told about that terrible destruction?'

'He looked shocked.'

'He looked shocked. Well, well. Please go on. What happened next?'

'He asked if he could see the kitchen.'

'The kitchen? Did he say why?'

'No, I don't think he did.'

'So you took him there?'

'Yes. I left him there with one of the maids and returned to my studio. A few minutes later the guards entered and found the bag under one of my tables.'

'You saw them find it?'

'Yes.'

'Did they open it in front of you?'

'Yes.'

'And what was in it?'

'Weapons.'

'Now let me ask you this. From the time he first entered your studio to the time you left him with the maid in the kitchen, did you lose sight of him? Did you leave him on his own, even for just a few minutes?'

'No.'

'Were you surprised that the guards found the bag in your room?'

'Yes.'

'Now I want you to think carefully before you answer my next question. Can you honestly tell the court without any doubt at all that Mordec son of Hauk had never entered your studio until the moment that afternoon when he came there in response to your invitation?'

'Well, I'm pretty sure he'd never been there before. I had to show him the way into the castle.'

'But he *might* have been there before?'

'I suppose it's possible.'

'Might he have been there earlier that day? I mean, if he crossed the ford at noon and took say twenty minutes to reach the castle, wouldn't he have had time to go to your studio, hide the bag, and go away again only to appear a little later empty-handed in the courtyard?'

'I don't think ...'

'I'm asking you—is it possible?'

'It's *possible* but ...'

'Thank you. No more questions.'

The Earl told Mel he could go. Mel cast a quick encouraging look at Mordec before he left the court.

'Now,' said the Earl, 'the Prosecution will sum up its case.'

'My Lord and learned judges. Nobody who has heard the evidence can doubt that a plot was hatched and in part carried out by at least one Viking boy. I do not want you to suppose that our Viking neighbors, co-signatories to the Treaty of Fairplay, were as a group in any way responsible for it. What reason could there be for them to want to end the peaceful co-existence we have enjoyed for five years now? If they had a reason, would they need to be devious about it—to send in a mere boy to do violence here while they sail off for a week's trading? It would be a cunning plan, to wait and see if the boy brought it off, be ready to deny any involvement if he didn't, or to take advantage of the results if he did. But no. I accuse them of nothing. It is far more likely that the boy himself, with a boy's foolishness, wanting to prove himself as a fighting man, planned the mischief all by himself. I suggest that he entered the earldom some time before Master de Gustybuss saw him in the main courtyard of the castle, hid the bag in the first hiding-place he saw which happened to be Master de Gustybuss's studio, then went away and returned empty-handed. When he asked to be shown round the castle he hoped to discover where the Earl was that afternoon. The only action he could take single-handed that would put this land in peril would be a fatal attack on the Earl himself.'

A commotion broke out among the spectators at the back of the hall. 'Death to him! Strangle him! Drown him in the Bog! To the Brockalee with him!' voices cried. Mordec looked round to see the excited and angry faces. Angriest was his jailer, Mistress Pillikin.

'Silence, please,' the Earl begged.

'Fortunately the arms were found and the attack prevented. Now, no one can be punished for a crime he did not commit, even if there is good reason to believe that he intended to commit it. The prisoner is not on trial for what he intended to do but what he did. He did not harm the Earl. But he brought arms into the earldom, an offence for which the punishment is death by strangulation and immersion in the Bog of Brockalee. But—'

The crowd, greatly excited by these words, began to shout again, even louder. Again the Earl begged them to be silent, and slowly they became still.

'But, I was trying to say, custom allows the court to be merciful. So I ask the court for mercy on the grounds that the prisoner is only a boy.'

The crowd groaned its disappointment.

'In recommending mercy I have to name an alternative punishment. I suggest that he be made bondsman for life, to labour in the Earldom of Linkard without wages for the rest of his days. The work that in my opinion he would best be suited to, if he really can read and write, is as assistant to Father Donlock in the library. There is every chance that he might become a Christian, and by sparing a life we would have saved a soul. Also, as a final thought, your lordships might feel that there would be a certain poetic justice in the boy's having to care for the remnant of the great collections of books which his people destroyed.'

'The library?' Mordec thought. 'For life? A warm castle, books and a teacher, new friends—if only Mom would come and live here too, or at least visit me every summer with Dad …' He suddenly felt that being found guilty would not be a disaster after all.

'And how does the Defense sum up its case?' the Earl asked.

Master Hitchem rose and walked briskly towards Mordec. He folded his arms, and smiled, first at the prisoner, then at the judges.

'My Lord and learned judges,' he said, 'I ask you to consider that the prisoner is a foreigner. He comes from another country. Another tradition. I am not saying that his people and their customs are inferior. Perish the thought! I'm saying that it behooves us, gentlemen, to take into our consideration the customs of his own people. What view would they take of a crime committed by what the Prosecutor has called "only a boy"? I can tell you this because I happen to know. It's most curious.'

He went to stand in front of Mordec, and bent backwards to look up at his face. 'It seems they consider a boy of the prisoner's age to be half-a-man. Their boys, these half-men as they call them, sail with them in half-a-ship—I am using their words, I beg you to remember—wearing half-size armour and equipped with half-size weapons. Perhaps they expect them to half obey the law?'

The crowd tittered. It was plain to Mordec that this mockery of his height, and of all Vikings as big and stupid, was to entertain the crowd, not to soften the judges.

'So this half-a-man,' Bill went on, 'crosses our frontier half-bearing arms—that is, he does not carry them openly and threateningly, but conceals them in a bag.'

Again the crowd tittered appreciatively. But the judges, Mordec noticed, kept their grave faces.

'What I urge the court to do in this case is apply a punishment to a Viking that the Vikings themselves will understand. If you do, the punishment of one of their own will not rouse them to rage, will not provoke them to break the Treaty and descend upon us with their ruthless might.' At this the judges looked alarmed.

'To save ourselves from the fury of the Northmen, let's think as they think, let's fit our ideas to theirs. For half-a-man who is half-a-criminal, let's decree half-a-punishment. Not strangulation, my lords, but half-strangulation. Not immersion in the Bog of Broackalee, but half-immersion in the Bog of Brockalee.'

The crowd, led by Mistress Pillikin, roared its approval. The judges fell to whispering. They leaned close to each other, turned their heads this way and that as sharply as birds, and their lips rustled like dry brown leaves on November branches.

Bill returned to his chair and smiled at Mordec as though he had done him an inspired favour. Surely, Mordec thought, the judges would see that that was a worse punishment than the Prosecutor had asked for? Surely the Earl, who seemed to be a just and kindly man, would not allow him to be tortured to death as the People's Friend demanded?

The judges opened great books and pored over them. Their sharp noses moved along the lines. They clapped their hands for their clerks and sent them to fetch more books, and there was a dashing in and out of the doors beyond the table, a dragging about of open volumes, a shaking of heads, a thrust or two of Latin, and despite all the bustle round him, or because of it, the Earl dropped off to sleep. He was woken by the other judges shaking him. They murmured, they gestured, they pointed to the books. At last he nodded his agreement and they all sat down and looked sternly at Mordec.

'Prisoner,' the Earl said, in a most sympathetic tone, 'the Prosecutor has asked for mercy in your case. But the law is clear. No mercy for your crime. Give me the book.' The judge sitting beside him pushed an open volume in front of his eyes and he read. 'Death shall be the punishment for man, woman, boy, girl, bond or free who enters the earldom bearing arms; for beast of the hearth, the farm or the wilderness; for fowl wild or tame; for fish of sweet water or of brine; all living things except a knight who may choose instead to fight for his life.'

One of the other judges then spoke. He was a very stout man with three chins, but his nose was small and pointed, so it looked like a beak on an owl's face. He leant forward and asked in all seriousness: 'You have not, I take it, been dubbed a knight by any monarch in Christendom? You may speak.'

Mordec snatched his thoughts back from trying to picture how beasts, birds or fishes could bear arms, and seized the moment.

'No, but I wasn't there,' he gabbled, 'when Knefrod told the others about the treaty and the law, and I didn't pack the bag and I never asked Kol to carry it, he—'

'That is what you say, Mordec son of Hauk,' said the stout judge, 'but the Defense called only one witness. No one has come forward to say you were somewhere else at the time this Knefrod was telling the others about the treaty and the law. And no one has told us that he saw anyone else pack the bag.'

Mordec tried to think fast what he should say to this while he had the chance. Wasn't it equally telling that no had come forward to say that they'd seen him carrying the bag? But his moment to speak was past and gone.

'So now,' the Earl said, 'we come to the plea of the Defense. 'We understand the argument that we should respect the customs of other nations.'

On this point Mordec knew just what to say. If the customs of the Vikings were to be respected in the court he was not yet old enough to stand trial. 'In that case—' he began.

'Quiet, please,' the Earl said. 'It is also right that we should be flexible where the law might be eased without being disobeyed. But here it cannot be eased. The law is perfectly plainly stated. Unless you can prove that you did not act in deliberate defiance of it, the facts as proved by the Prosecution stand against you. The penalty is also plainly stated. Death by strangulation and immersion in the bog. So we cannot do as the Defense asks. I must add that in my own view Master Hitchem's idea of a specially merciful way for a boy to be put to death is a good deal worse than the usual way.' For the first time the Earl sounded harsh when he said these words. Mordec looked at Bill. The People's Friend was sitting in his place smiling, and without the smile fading a jot, he heaved a deep sigh and spread his hands out towards Mordec as if to say, 'I'm sorry, I meant well, I did my best, but what can I do with these hard men of the law?'

The Earl went on: 'Mordec son of Hauk, you are sentenced to be returned to your place of confinement and to be taken from there at first light tomorrow to the Bog of Brockalee where you shall be strangled and sunk. And may God have mercy on your soul.'

'But—but—' Mordec shouted in protest.

The Earl, who had turned away, looked back at him. 'Produce a witness before tomorrow morning and I'll hear your appeal,' he said, in his kind tone.

Two guards hustled Mordec down the hall. Almost everyone in the crowd shook a fist or spat in his direction. He saw Mistress Pillikin hurrying off, needing to get to the tower ahead of him and unlock the door.

He glanced up at the gallery. He thought he saw Jessica shake her head slightly. If so, what could she be meaning to tell him now—that there was nothing she could do, or that he mustn't give up hope?

Out through the great double doors he was marched, and down the vaulted passage where the armed platoon was waiting for him. The portcullis was raised, the drawbridge dropped. Over they tramped and on they went to the grim grey tower.

yaremouth wic

Lily reached Yaremouth the day before Mordec's trial—if Jessica had rightly guessed when it would be. For all Lily knew it was over and done with, he'd been found guilty, and was now lying dead in the Bog of Brockalee. But she told herself it was useless thinking that. She must do what she'd come to do.

The market was on the edge of the town. She saw pens of cattle, pigs, and slaves. Most of the slaves were young men and boys, thickly built but pale. Their heads had been shaved to a grey-blue stubble. On a few of their pates the razor had spared an odd lock of hair to hang down over one ear. Their cheeks were streaked with pigment, blood-red and bruise-blue. Spiked leather collars were buckled round their necks. They were very noisy with cussing and swearing, and seemed to have almost no other words. But Lily could tell they were not foreign but came from somewhere in these islands. Their only garment was a pair of goat trousers, held up by narrow chains over their shoulders and across their backs. Their feet were bare, the soles as hard as horn.

The few women and girls among them were almost as hefty and muscular. They too had shaven heads, or cropped hair stiffened with pigfat. Their short tunics were dust-streaked and grease-dirty, and some of them carried babies decorated with blue patches on their pale pink skins.

They were not chained together, and hardly guarded at all. Older men were selling them who looked much the same as the slaves, thick and shaven-headed, but they wore more clothes and their faces were browner and more leathery. They wandered about, stood in the shade to chat, or sat in the dust and drank from stoneware bottles. Any slave who wanted to could easily have got away. 'They must want to be slaves!' Lily thought with contempt and disgust.

'What are they good for?' she asked one of the leathery slavers.

'Nothing much,' the seller admitted cheerfully. 'But they're all dirt cheap. Knock-down prices. Y'can use them for knockin' down if yer like.' And he laughed at his own joke, choked on his phlegm and spat in the dust.

'Would they do for soldiers?' Lily asked herself. She bent down to look closer at one of them, and he looked up at her, wrinkled his nose and bared his teeth—two in the top jaw, widely spaced, and a few in the lower, all of them chipped and stained and leaning higgledy-piggledy in thick beds of swollen gums. He may have been about to say something, to shout an oath or an insult at her, but a look in her eye, fierce and unflinching, took him by surprise and silenced him. She answered her own question: 'No— not soldiers. Not even brigands. "Good for nothing" is right—except perhaps lunch for the little lioness.'

On she went, scanning the crowd. As well as towns-folk there were farmers in wide straw hats, foresters in green, ladies attended by pages, some knights, many priests, a few foreigners but no Vikings among them. She must search the busy market, the harbour, the town itself, find them within the next two hours and persuade them to start sailing back—all except Gus who must ride with her.

Maelstrom kept his head high although the ride had been long and hard, and many a farmer turned his head to watch him go by. But Roman Ruin hung his head wearily and had to blow the rising dust out of his irritated nostrils.

Weapons caught Lily's eye as she passed the tables spread with wares, but she didn't pause again. She found the Vikings among stacks of wool-bales. It was easy enough to pick them out from the rest, they were such big men, most of them with yellow hair and beards. She saw the boys too, Gus first, the tallest. When she was still some distance away she put her cupped hands to her mouth and shouted his name.

He and the other boys looked up, startled. The surprise on Gus's face changed to a smile of pleasure when he saw who was calling him, and changed again when he saw Roman Ruin. He hurried towards Lily.

'You're not going to sell Roman Ruin are you? You said I could keep him …'

'No, I haven't come to sell anything. I've come to fetch you. Mordec's been arrested in the earldom and they're going to try him and if he's found guilty they'll kill him. You've got to come and save him.'

'Mordec? Locked up? Guilty? What of? You'd better come and explain. I'll get the other boys—and
Big Olaf, and Harvald the Armourer.'

Lily wanted to use up as little time as possible on
explanations, but she saw that only by getting them
to understand how bad Mordec's predicament was
could she persuade them to hurry back and save him.
So when Big Olaf said that they should all go into
the ale-house and sit down with a drink and hear
the story, she felt she had no choice but to do as
they wished.

They started drinking at once, and talking about
the trade they'd done, and laughing as they told
each other what bargains they'd struck, what mis-
takes they'd made, what they'd seen and heard. It
was some minutes before Big Olaf and Harvald gave
her their attention. Then Big Olaf lifted her on to
the ale-house table and called out, 'Silence! The little
queen has a story to tell us.'

Standing above them, her head almost touching
the ceiling, Lily said: 'Mordec's been arrested in the
earldom. They say he went there with a bagful of
weapons. He didn't, I know. Someone put his sword
and things into his bag and hid it in the castle. But
they'll bring him to trial, and if he's found guilty
they'll strangle him and push him into the Bog of
Brockalee. You must come and save him. There isn't
much time.'

The men were silent for a minute or more, drinking
and thinking. The boys stared at Lily, half-formed
questions chasing each other in and out of their heads.

Gunnar the Sailmaker said: 'But he's only a boy. Boys under fifteen can't commit crime.'

'Under *your* law that may be. In the earldom if they're found guilty they're killed,' Lily said impatiently.

Hakon said: 'When they come to kill Mordec he'll fight them. He can't win, but he'll go to the Hall of the Heroes. He'll be the youngest hero ever. Hauk his father will be proud of him. The skalds will make up a saga about him.'

'But Estrid his mother will not soon forget her grief and rage if she loses her only son,' Big Olaf said.

Lily put her hands on her hips and glared down at them with her most queenly air. 'I'm not asking you to do it for nothing,' she said. 'I know how things are done. I'll pay you.'

Hakon laughed and the others joined in. What will you pay us?'

'A heap of gold.'

The laughter died down. 'What gold?' Svend the Dyer asked.

'Lots of it. I told Mordec about it. I told him to tell you that you could have it if you'd go away and never come back.'

'Done!' Hakon shrilled in a woman's voice, then added in his deepest tone, *'if* there's enough to fill a thousand ships!' And they all laughed again.

'It's not *that* much but it is a lot. And I'll give it to you if you'll come and save Mordec.'

Again there was silence as they thought about the gold.

Then Big Olaf said, 'If we enter the earldom with weapons to fight the Earl's guard, we'll be breaking the treaty.'

'Yes,' Lily said. You must fight the Earl's guard. The treaty must be broken.'

'You'd like that, wouldn't you, Lily?' Gus said. 'You want the Earl to raise an army and make war on us, don't you?'

'Yes,' Lily said.

'Is that why you've made up this story?' Gunnar the Sailmaker said.

'I haven't made it up! It's true. Oh, how can I make you believe me!'

'I believe you,' Gus said. 'Poor old Mordec—I don't s'pose he's laughing now. But you never know with Mordec. Maybe he did take the weapons into the earldom.'

'But what would he take them there *for*?' Eric wondered.

'Especially as Knefrod told you all not to and what would happen if you did,' Harvald said.

'He wasn't there when Knefrod told us,' Gus remembered.

'Where was he?' Hakon asked his son.

'He'd gone fishing when—'

Lily leapt down from the table, took Gus by the wrist and tried to pull him towards the door.

'Come and tell them that. I brought Roman Ruin so you could ride back with me. If you come and tell them that, maybe they'll believe he's innocent— come on—'

'We'll all come back and tell them if you'll tell us now where the gold is,' Svein the Carter said.

'I'll tell you when you've saved him. Come on, come on—' she pulled at Gus and looked round desperately at the faces of the Vikings. 'Gus *must* ride with me.'

Gus let her drag him towards the door, but Hakon took hold of his other arm and pulled him back. 'If I let Gus come with you, and if what he says saves Mordec, maybe you'll never tell us where the gold is hidden,' he said teasingly.

'Yes,' said Svein the Carter, more seriously, 'how can we trust you to tell us where the gold is if we save him first?'

'You don't have to trust me,' she answered, almost choking with exasperation. 'Mordec knows where the gold is. I told him. If you free him, he'll tell you where it is.' She tugged at Gus with all her might. '*Let him go!*' Gus was pulled this way and that between Lily who turned red in the face with the effort, and Hakon, who used one brawny arm to play his son out and pull him in again, and the other to lift a jug of ale to his lips— Lily let go of Gus suddenly, so that he staggered on one foot and crashed against his father before regaining his balance. She rushed up to Hakon and punched and pushed him, then with one swift movement drew her dagger from the back of her belt and shouted, 'If you don't come with me Gus, I swear I'll scar you and your father!' Harvald took hold of her arm with one hand and twisted it slightly to make her drop her weapon. She bared her teeth, took a step back, and reached for her short silver sword. With a look that was both inviting and menacing, she slashed it through the air. Horsa leapt forward, sword in hand and a cold watchfulness in his eyes.

But the men only smiled. Big Olaf and Hakon laughed. Harvald drew his own sword, struck hers from her hand with one quick upward blow, then picked it up and examined it with interest. 'Oddsbods. This could be the work of my own father,' he said. 'Horsa, come and see.'

Horsa, disappointed though he was not to be fighting an English resister at last, looked closely at the hilt and ran his fingers along the flat of the blade. 'It's beautiful,' he said.

'It belonged to a Viking,' Lily shouted furiously, holding up her fists.

They all looked at her and she dropped her arms. They were waiting for her to explain, and since she couldn't force them to do her bidding, she felt there was no choice but to try talking again.

'His name was Osvald son of Olvir,' she said. 'He came with Eyiolf the Bald. They plundered the gold I've been telling you about. We buried it. And they took my mother away.'

At the name of Eyiolf the Bald their faces became thoughtful. Harvald put his sword away and said briskly. 'Well, Olaf, shall we try and get Mordec out of the Earl's prison? We promised Hauk we'd look after his son.'

'We'll start back in the ships today,' Big Olaf announced to the whole company. 'We'll parley with the Earl before someone persuades him that Mordec was sent in by us to break the treaty. If we find out that someone *has* been up to such tricks, we'll know who set Mordec up. We'll get hold of the rat and scorch the truth out of him.'

'You're coming back?' Lily asked. 'All of you?'

'We are,' the Sailmaker said.

'Hurry then.'

'I don't know about hurrying,' Big Olaf said dubiously.

'The wind isn't with us. We can't be sure how long the voyage will take.'

They gave her back her dagger and sword. She went out through the low door and untethered Maelstrom. She put her hand on Roman Ruin's lead rope, but glanced back at the door and let it go. No one was standing there to see her off. She smiled to herself, and leaving Roman Ruin where he was, mounted and rode off through the market. Now and then she turned to look behind her.

When she reached the Roman road she started northward, but stopped at the first milestone to wait. Barely five minutes had passed when she heard the clop of galloping hooves, and moments later saw the horse and rider. Gus sped past her, grinning, and she urged Maelstrom after Roman Ruin. Gus would never beat her in any race, she vowed. And, anyway, no horse in the world could move faster than Maelstrom.

the heart of a viking

Father Donlock was not a friendly man, but he was just, unselfish and dutiful. Late in the afternoon he set out for the Tower of Doom with a phial of holy water in his pocket to do what he could for the condemned criminal. But first he had to call on the Keeper of the Key.

Mistress Pillikin opened her door a crack in response to his knock. Seeing who it was, she opened it wider and said, pursing her lips, 'Ooh, Father, what can I do for you?'

'Please come with me and let me into the Tower of Doom for a few minutes so that I can console the prisoner.'

'Ooh, that is good of you, Father. The poor boy. I'll come at once.'

She lamented Mordec's fate all the way to the tower. 'I'll wait for you here, Father,' she said as she unlocked the lower door. She handed the key to the blue-feather. He would climb the long screw of stairs and unlock the door at the top.

As soon as Father Donlock saw Mordec, he came straight to the point. 'It's my duty to offer to baptize you,' he said.

'Is that some form of torture?' Mordec asked.

'Not at all. Quite the opposite. It's the best thing in the world.'

'What happens?'

'Well. Quite a lot should happen. I should first teach you about Christianity, but there isn't enough time.'

'If you've got a book about it—' Mordec suggested hopefully.

Father Donlock thought about this. 'Can you read Latin?'

'No.'

'I thought not. So I've decided to go against my own idea of what is right and offer to baptize you without teaching you. All you have to do is say that you are willing. Then I just put a little of this water on your forehead and say a few words.'

Mordec eyed the very small phial that the priest held up. 'Couldn't you make it a lot of water, enough to pour all over me?'

'No. This is holy water. I use only as much as is necessary.'

'It won't help then,' Mordec said.

'Help what?'

'Help me to get clean.'

'It'll cleanse your soul.'

Footsteps reached the top of the stairs. The door swung inwards and there stood Master Bill Hitchem, smiling. Father Donlock sighed. 'I'll go. But I'll be back in the morning. If you change your mind then, I'll have the holy water with me.'

'Good-night, Father,' Bill said sweetly.

'Hardly,' the priest replied. Bill stared after him with a questioning look. Then he smiled again and went to the window. The sun was descending and beginning to redden and the colour was reflected in the Bog of Brockalee as in a black mirror.

'It's not far to the place of execution,' Bill said, gazing out. 'But you know, you don't have to see that as your destiny. *I happen to know* that *you* know where a whole heap of gold lies hidden. Now if you were to tell me exactly where it is, I believe I could find a witness or two who could save you.'

'Why didn't you find them in time for the trial?'

'I lacked the resources.'

'But you knew Kol was lying?'

Bill ignored the question. 'You must listen to what I'm offering you. It's your only chance, you see.'

'You didn't really try to defend me properly,' Mordec said.

Bill looked at Mordec, at the size of him, and realized that if he turned violent, as they said Vikings often did without cause or warning, he could do a fair amount of damage with his bare hands to a defenseless peace-loving man. The barbarian must be made to understand that Bill was his friend.

He launched into rapid speech. 'What I want to make clear is that if the court had decided to punish you as the Prosecution had asked, certainly yes you would have been allowed to live, but I can assure you that your life would have been hard, very hard indeed. The only good thing about it would have been that at least in this country bondsmen are cared for by Mistress Pillikin and myself in an institution known as Bond House. It must be remembered that there was a time not so long ago when men and boys in bonded labour had to live with their masters—as the women and girls still do, absolutely at their mercy. It's entirely due to myself that conditions have improved for the males. I only wish I could do the same for the females. All I can say is that the policy is in place, the process has begun, and in the fullness of time the goal will be reached. I'm not resting on my laurels. I don't give up. I got the government to build one Bond House, and in time I'll get it to build another. I've made it absolutely clear to the Earl that that is the right direction to go. I'm not ashamed to admit frankly that I'm an idealist, and I won't rest until the government looks after everybody equally. The people have a right to our care. Now what was I saying? Oh yes. Of course I would have seen that you were well looked after. I think also that it would have done a lot of good to you personally. You might have learnt real community spirit. But—'

'But?' Mordec said. 'So why didn't you agree that I should be a bond servant? Why did you ask the court to have me half strangled and half choked in mud?'

'If *you* will only tell me,' Bill said brightly, 'what I want to know, I myself will appeal for your sentence to be changed to life in Bond House. I can promise you that.'

'So you wanted to scare me into telling you where this gold is that you say I know about?'

'Listen,' Bill said, 'and try to understand. I don't want the gold for *myself*. It's for widows and orphans. Does the plight of the poor mean nothing to you? Have you no heart at all?'

'I won't tell you anything,' Mordec said firmly. He lay down on his straw, put the bundled-up blanket under his head, and looked up at the rafters.

'I just don't know how to make you see sense,' Bill said. 'Anyway, I'll give you one last chance. I'll come to the bogside tomorrow morning. Perhaps when the executioner's standing beside you with the cord in his hand, you'll see things differently. I hate to see a young lad throw his life away for want of a little heart and an itsy-bit of community spirit.'

Mordec sat up suddenly and looked hard at Bill. 'Did you tell Kol to put the weapons in the bag and hide it in the castle?'

'Of course I didn't. *Would* I do a thing like that?'

Yes,' Mordec said. 'You would. I know now why you didn't try to defend me. You set me up, didn't you? You and Kol?'

Bill's smile faded. 'What sort of person do you think I am? And who're you to point a finger? A boy who doesn't care a rap for widows and orphans!' He spoke more and more heatedly, but suddenly remembered his training in charm, and smiled again. 'Now don't let yourself get too miserable. If you feel miserable in the night and need someone to come and console you just shout to the guards below that you want to see me and they'll get the message to me. I'll come, I promise, whatever the hour. Good-night.

Sleep well. No need to thank.' And with a hasty wave he left.

The guard who'd been waiting on the landing pulled the door shut but didn't lock it, so when they'd gone Mordec opened it again, pulling it into to the room very slowly in case its creaking should reach the ears of the guards below. He found that his shoulders almost filled the width of the doorway. He stepped behind the open door, lifted his joined hands above his head and brought them down hard on an imaginary guard's back.

'They won't take me without a fight,' he told his absurdly small water jug and bowl, and went on to explain to them: 'I'll knock down the first one who comes in, get his sword, finish him off, and be ready to fight the next one.'

A loud caw interrupted him. A raven settled on the stone sill of the window. It reminded Mordec of what Bill had said about the heads popping up in the bog and the ravens picking out the eyes, and he froze. Vividly he imagined the cord tightening round his throat and thick black mud closing over his face. For a few moments he was gripped by fear. Then he folded his arms on his chest, smiled disdainfully at the bird and told it, 'I'll not be easy meat for you or them. I'll fight and I'll win. Stupid thing! Don't you know that I'm a Viking?'

The raven lifted its wings, glared at him with its beady eyes and flew off, cawing loudly, as though reporting Mordec's challenge to all the other ravens who haunted the air between the bog and the tower, watching for carrion.

nightcap

'Now, son, about this gold you were waffling on about,' Knefrod said to Kol as he deftly skinned the buck he had brought home on a farmer's cart. 'Where did you say it is?'

'I don't know exactly,' Kol said. 'I only know it's somewhere in the ruins of a Roman fort not too far from here.'

'I know where the Roman fort is,' Knefrod said. 'No one ever said gold was hidden there. Who told you about it?'

'I heard that girl Lily talking about it.'

'So she knows where it is, hm? She and who else?'

'She told Mordec.'

'Mordec? Why?'

'She wanted him to tell all of us so that we'd take the gold and go away. But if you and I could get it for ourselves before the others come back—'

'Why didn't Mordec tell us about it?'

'I think he was waiting until the others came back from the wic. And then he got arrested. The thing is—they're going to strangle him tomorrow morning. Someone should go and see him before that happens.'

'Go and see him then. What are you waiting for?'

'He'd never tell me. He hates me.'

'But he'd tell me, wouldn't he? I mean to say, if he was going to tell Olaf the Shipbuilder and Harvald the Armourer, why not me? If the whole idea was for us to have the gold—?'

'He wouldn't tell you because—well, because you're my dad.'

'Then who else knows where the gold is?'

'Lily told Mordec that her grandmother knows.'

'And that's all—Mordec, Lily, and her granny?'

Kol nodded.

'We'll ask Lily,' Knefrod said. 'She wanted us to know anyway, so she'll tell us.'

'I think she'll only tell us now if we rescue Mordec. She likes Mordec.'

'I know. She came here a couple of days ago and asked Egil to rescue him. She said something to him about giving us gold if we'd rescue Mordec. Of course Egil said we couldn't go and fight the Earl's guard. Even if we wanted to there aren't enough of us. So then she asked where the others were and he told her. So come to think of it she's probably ridden off to Yaremouth to hurry them home. If she has, there's nobody around here to ask but the granny. Well, when I've finished this I'll go and get it out of the old girl.'

'D'you think she'll tell you?'

'I'll persuade her. One way or another. I'm not going to let some old lady stand between me and a fortune.'

'You know where she lives?'

'Goosegarth. I've never been there but I know where it is.'

'Can I come with you?'

'No. When I go to talk to a lady I don't want you there spoiling my efforts. I've got a way with the girls, young or old. You'll be the same one day, but not yet.'

***

When Knefrod arrived at Goosegarth after a brisk walk, he thought he'd go quietly into the house and surprise the old lady. His sword was on his hip, but he'd brought no shield. He was expecting no interference. 'If dogs or geese attack,' he thought, 'I'll slash my way through them.' But neither goose nor dog came to intercept the stranger.

Knefrod found the entrance door of the house slightly open. He flung it wide and bellowed, 'Anyone home? Here has arrived Knefrod the Viking. I demand that the mistress of the house receive me at once!' He stood and listened for an answer. Not a sound came back to him.

He strode in, shouting, 'Come on, where are you, Granny? It's no good hiding. I'll not hurt you if you do as I say. Now don't be a silly old cow! Come on, creep out of whatever hole you're skulking in!'

On the table were platters of fruit and garlands of white lilies. He reached for a sloe, and as he did so became aware that a lady was standing quietly in the shadows beyond the table, watching him.

'You Lily's grandmother?' he asked, his mouth full.

'I am Queen Bertha,' she replied in her quiet husky tones. 'To what do I owe the honor of your visit?'

192

Knefrod planted his feet apart, put his hand on the hilt of his sword, spat out the sloe-pit on to the floor, smiled the smile of a hungry wolf and said, 'Hullo, Gran! Can we talk?'

'About something in particular?' Queen Bertha inquired.

'Lily sent a message to us, but we never got it. Not all of it. I've come to get it.'

'And what would the message be about?'

'Gold. She wanted us to know where some gold is hidden.'

'Oh?'

'What's so surprising? You knew, didn't you?'

'Look about you, sir. Do you think that if we had gold we'd live like this? This is not how we English live when we are rich. You must have seen how the Earl lives over the border at Linkard Castle. No—if it's gold you want, you've come to the wrong place.'

'Now listen to me,' Knefrod said, his smile, such as it was, leaving his face, his grip tightening on his sword. 'I happen to know that Lily told Mordec son of Hauk to come and tell us where the gold is. She told him she wants us to have it.'

'Amazing!' said the Queen. 'You had better ask her about it.'

'Is she here?'

'No, she's gone away for a few days. If you're in a hurry, why don't you ask Mordec son of Hauk where it is?'

'He's not easy to get to.'

'So I hear. Are you planning to get him out of that tower?'

Knefrod ignored the question. He pulled out a chair, sat down, and said 'Come nearer. Let me look at you.'

Queen Bertha came softly out of the shadows but kept the table between them. He saw how tall and slender she was, and straight as a column. A silk mantle the colour of rain covered her from throat to floor. Knefrod thought, 'There's more serpent in her than woman,' and he felt a twinge of something that might have been fear had he not been a Viking. To stop the small shiver deep inside him he barked at her, 'Come round here, don't be frightened.'

He slapped his knee. 'Come and sit *here,* old girl, and we'll soon be laughing together.'

Queen Bertha was silent just long enough to let his words hover about his own ears and tell him how rude he was. Then she took up a jug and a cup. 'Will you have wine?' she asked in her lowest smoothest tones.

'Yeah,' he said.

She poured the wine and rather ceremoniously, with both hands, held out the cup across the table. He had to rise to take it. He grinned, looking now more like a sheep than a wolf.

'Come on, you too, sweetheart. I won't drink alone when I'm in the company of ladies.'

She bowed her head, took a cup from the table, and raised it. 'I drink to your getting all that you deserve,' she murmured, and set her cup down.

'And I to your beautiful eyes,' he said with a certain coarse gallantry which was the best imitation of courtesy he could manage. He drank and sat suddenly.

'More?' Queen Bertha asked softly. He held out his cup, she filled it, and again he drained it, tipping his head far back when it was empty and feeling with his tongue for the last intoxicating drop. He set the cup down with an unsteady hand, and it fell over. Leaning on the table he tried to rise but fell in a heap on the floor.

'Now,' he mumbled, finding that his tongue had grown thick and was getting in the way of his words. 'Where izh … where'zh …?' A deep snore began to grind in his chest.

'Sir Baz,' Queen Bertha called softly, and from behind a tapestry Sir Baz stepped out. He went up to the sleeping Viking, stared down at him for a moment, then uttered a short sharp laugh without for a moment altering the gloomy look on his face.

'I'll get Walter.'

While he was gone, Queen Bertha poured the remains of the wine from the jug into an earthenware bottle which she stoppered securely.

When Sir Baz came in with Walter she pointed to the big snoring body of the hunter and asked, 'Where do you think—?'

'The pigsty?' Walter suggested.

She nodded.

Walter said, 'When a geezer makes a noise like that, that's where he belongs. Maybe my pigs will like him, and maybe they won't.'

He and Sir Baz took Knefrod by the legs and shoulders and heaved him through the hall and out to the sty in the barn, where they dumped him on a heap of straw which had been clean that morning but wasn't now. Hearing his snorts, the pigs came to root about him and join in, until there was such a merry chorus serenading the farmyard that the geese gave voice too, and the donkey and the dogs and the goat, and none of them stopped until the sun went down.

* * *

Queen Bertha came out into the twilight.

'Walter, coax the roan between the shafts. Pile the red foxes. I'll drive myself to Linkard Castle to talk to the Earl. When our guest wakes let him find his way round the little lioness. If he comes out alive, let him go. But keep his weapon.'

Her chariot was merely the farm haycart, and the roan was no longer sprightly, but when Queen Bertha was seated on the high bench covered with the long-haired pelts of foxes, and the reins were gathered up in her ringed hands, anyone could see that this was a royal conveyance; more royal yet when her attendant white knight, Sir Baz, fell in behind it, his white steed's head arched high, and on his upright lance a white pennant fluttering in the evening breeze.

The Earl was in his nightgown and nightcap of scarlet flannel, garments which he'd allowed Mel de Gustybuss to design for him, and was sipping warm milk at the open window of his countinghouse when his visitor was announced and admitted. She was

196

alone. Sir Baz had gone to a higher chamber to pay his respects to Lady Jessica.

Bertha stepped in and stood regally just inside his door, stretching out her arms. The Earl picked up his long nightrobe and crossed the room to her. He kissed her hand ceremoniously, then put his arms about her shoulders and hugged her.

'Bertha! What a nice surprise.'

In the candlelight she seemed to the old Earl to look just as she had when they'd been as young as Lily and Jessica were now.

'Reggie, my old friend. Are you truly surprised? Weren't you expecting a visitor or two on the night before an execution?'

'I feel bad about the boy, but the law—'

'Is the law. I know, my dear, I know.'

'Of course if new witnesses were to come forward … Even one more for the Defense would do. The Prosecution's case was not good. If he'd brought the bag to the castle earlier, why had no one been found who saw him bring it? Hitchem should have said that. It seemed to me he didn't want to save the boy.'

'Ah, that's a cunning clown,' Bertha said. 'And his tongue's an acrobat in its own right.'

'And then,' Reggie went on, pursuing his thoughts, 'there is the question of who left that note where the guards would have to find it. Whoever did that set the whole thing up. Hitchem should have tried to get to the bottom of it before the case came to court.'

'Is there someone you suspect?'

'I can't think who would have a reason to do it, unless it was to wreck the treaty.'

'My granddaughter wants to do that. But she likes this Viking boy.'

'I asked Father Donlock who else had come to the library that afternoon. And d'you know what he said? "Only Bill Hitchem".'

'He'd frame anyone for gain. But what could he have gained?'

'I wonder. Well, if anyone comes forward to swear that Mordec left the Viking village alone and empty-handed, or that another person packed the bag or carried it here, or that Kod or Kol, whatever his name is, lied about anything, it would be enough to override his testimony. If anyone can show that any part of the case against Mordec isn't true, I'll put off the execution. My door and my ears are open right up to the last minute. The law should never be used to serve injustice.'

'Lily's gone to find witnesses. But she needs time. Can you postpone the execution without new evidence, Reggie?'

The Earl shook his head. 'I'm sorry, m'dear.'

Queen Bertha did not give up and go away. She talked of other things for a while, things the two of them often talked about—shared memories, old friends, some of them dead. She made him laugh loudly three times and come near to weeping once. In the end she persuaded him to prepare a document which would suspend the sentence on Mordec and order the hearing of new evidence—but not to sign it. He would only do that, he said, if and when the new witnesses appeared and spoke.

Again Bertha talked for a while of the past. Then she said, 'Sign that document, Reggie. Then if time is short it will be ready. After all, if it's not to be used you can simply destroy it.'

He shook his head but gave in. 'It's perfectly senseless,' he said as he inked the tip of the quill and signed scratchily, 'but if it pleases you … There. I've done what you ask, m'dear. Caprice, sheer caprice. You always were capricious. All of you are—you, Gloria, Lily. Nothing but caprice.'

'Nothing else?'

He sighed. 'If you could have loved me long ago as I loved you!'

'We both wanted what we couldn't have. But tonight you've done this for me, and I thank you for it, Reggie. You're a dear good man.'

* * *

A sound of soft footsteps on the stone stairs? Mordec rose from the straw, crossed the moonlit room, opened the door and stood behind it. He had nothing to hit the guard with, but he'd have the advantage of surprise. He must get the man down on the floor and grab his sword.

The footsteps reached the landing and stopped just outside the door. Mordec readied himself, feet apart, fists raised. But whoever it was didn't stride in. A soft voice called, 'May I come in, please?'

It was a girl's voice. 'Lily!' he called, although the voice did not sound like hers—it was lighter and without the force and throatiness of Lily's.

'I'm sorry but I'm not Lily,' the voice said.

Mordec stepped out of his hiding place and looked to see who it was.

On the landing stood a figure with an oil lamp; someone who stood straight and tall, wrapped in a long white hooded cape. A small hand went up to the hood and pushed it back from a smiling face which he had seen before. 'Lady Jessica!'

'I bribed them with my silver rings to help me. They promised to leave this door unlocked. And to get the key from Pillikin to open the door downstairs, they told a fib. They said it was Father Donlock wanted it. Close the door and come and sit over here far from the door and the window.' They sat on the dusty floor against the stone wall.

'My father said that if witnesses come forward to say that Kol lied, he'll make the judges hear them. He'll stop your execution, and if the judges believe the new witnesses, you'll be let off altogether. My father's not a hard man, he wants to be fair, but he won't go against the law.'

'Do you believe that I never did what they say I did?'

'Yes.'

'Why?'

'Ally-pally came and told me everything he heard you telling Bill. He listened outside the door. I'll do anything I can to save you. So will Lily.'

'But what *can* you do? Or Lily?'

'She's gone to Yaremouth to find the men …'

'Lily has? To save me? But why?'

'I don't think it's because of justice or anything like that. With Lily it would always be because of the way she feels. She may do it because she likes you as a friend, and she may do it because she hates you as a Viking.'

'If she hates me as a Viking, why would she want to save me?'

'So she can use you to make war between us—between the earldom and the Vikings.'

'I see,' Mordec said. 'Of course. If they come and fight they'll be breaking the treaty.'

'Yes. That may be just what she wants. I know she hates the treaty. Her grandmother tried to get my father and all the earls and kings of England to fight the Vikings on land and sea. Now what I need you to tell me is—do you think they'd break the treaty to rescue you? If you think they'll come and fight, I must tell my father.'

Mordec got up from the floor and walked about, thinking. Finally he stopped, folded his arms on his chest and shook his head. 'No. My father asked Olaf the Shipbuilder and Harvald the Armourer to be my guardians. They gave their word. I think they'd try to help me, but not if it meant breaking the treaty.'

'That's good. Then the best thing Lily can do is find one or two of the boys who saw something and will come and tell the truth and show that Kol lied.'

'Yes, but—they couldn't get here in time, could they?'

'She may be on her way home now, with someone to speak for you.'

'But can they be here before morning?'

'They must be! I'll post look-outs at the ford. They'll light a bonfire to signal us at the castle when Lily crosses the river. I'll also have watchers on the ramparts and they'll fetch my father to hear the witnesses, and then he'll stop the execution. I must go now, but I'll see you again, no matter what. At the bog, if not before.'

'Will you bring me a sword?'

'If I were to put a sword in your hand you'd be guilty of the very thing they've condemned you for!'

'Then I must fight with my hands. If I can help it I won't die by being strangled and sunk in a bog— they'll have to put their swords through me.'

'I know you believe that if you die fighting you will go to the Hall of the Heroes.'

'So they say.'

'What will it be like there?'

'The way the priests and skalds describe it, it's one long meal. I wouldn't mind that, if the food's good. But I'd like to have some books.'

Jessica rose to her feet. 'I brought you a white roll and some cheese,' she said. She lifted the food, wrapped in oak leaves, out of a small pouch hanging at her side. 'And this,' she said, taking out a stone bottle. 'It's made by the Scots. They call it *water of life*. My father puts a spoonful in his milk at bedtime. He says it helps him sleep.' She set the bottle carefully on the floor, then she wrapped her cloak about her and pulled the hood over her head. 'I'll leave you the lantern too,' she said.

Mordec followed her to the door. He touched her arm as she was about to step out of the room and she turned to face him.

He said, 'You've done a lot for me. But I want to ask you a special favour. If I die tomorrow, will you get word to my mother and father about how I didn't do what I was found guilty of? And that I died fighting?—if I do, that is. I'm going to try. You could write it all down in a letter and send it to my mother with any of the boys except Kol. Or you could give it to Big Olaf or Harvald the Armourer. Will you?'

'I promise that if the worst comes to the worst I'll do all that. But let's keep on hoping. I believe you will be saved.' She left the room. He followed her on to the landing holding up the lantern to light her way down the first few steps. After that she had to feel her way down.

From the window he saw her emerge through the outer door, and Sir Baz coming forward to meet her, leading his own horse and another. He helped her to mount and they rode off. The moon lit their way—and would light Lily's way too, he thought.

One of the guards locked the door below. 'Stay in front of the door while I take this back to the Keeper of the Key,' he said, and his companion obeyed, standing stiffly, feet apart, his hand on the hilt of his sword.

'One man only now. I must think of a good reason to get him up here,' Mordec said aloud to himself.

He couldn't. But he tried calling anyway, 'Guard, guard! Come up here! Quickly!'

The guard looked up. 'What for?'

'I've got something for you.'

'Shut your trap,' the guard said, and returned to his post.

Mordec turned away from the window and the first thing he saw was the stone bottle. He pulled out the stopper and held the neck to his nose. Then he took a sip. 'Strange smell, strange taste,' he murmured. 'If anyone but Jessica had brought it I'd suspect it was a drug of some sort.' He filled his mouth, swallowed, and gasped. 'More like fire than water.' he said aloud. He took another swig, and rather to his own surprise began to sing: 'I had a wife, hm-hm-hm-hm, as white as alabaster, hm-hm-hm-hm-hm-hm-hm-hm, to keep it ever after.'

lioness

Knefrod stirred. He opened one eye and saw by torchlight a pair of eyes in a pink face close to his own. He looked at it through a veil of his own hair. His topknot had come undone.

'Funny,' he said aloud to the pig, 'a moment ago you looked different—brown and beautiful!'

The pig snorted and Knefrod sat up.

'Where am I?' he asked it.

Then he recognized the sty for what it was.

'The witch!' he said, meaning Queen Bertha.

He staggered to his feet, clutched his head, and wondered why a little wine should make him feel so dizzy, so dry in the mouth, so weak in the legs.

He staggered out of the sty and towards the open door of the barn. A growl stopped him. The creature that was making it was snarling at him, and looked so much like a lion with its square muzzle, its soft white beard, its tawny pelt, that he stood still and rubbed his eyes.

A lion? In these parts? He remembered that his son Kol had told him something about seeing 'the Lion of Loondal', but he hadn't believed him. When he opened his eyes again he saw that it really was a lioness, and she was drawing herself back in a posture

205

that told him she was readying herself to spring. He felt for his sword, but it wasn't there. Back in the sty he flung straw and pig-dung about, scrabbling to find his weapon. It wasn't there either.

He turned again to face the lioness, and this time he did not stagger. He moved like the hunter he was. With legs bent he took step after careful step, his body hunched, his arms and huge hands held ready to grab the beast if she should spring. And spring she did. He thrust out his arms, twisted his head away, tried to ward her off, but her paws caught him full on the chest and knocked him down. She stood snarling over him, her black-rimmed mouth so wide open that he saw not only the four big fangs, two above and two below, and her pink tongue, but right down into her throat, and he smelt her hot, meaty, angry breath.

He'd had close encounters with beasts of prey often before, but never as close as this. Yet she didn't seize him by the neck. Recovering his presence of mind, he squirmed backwards. The claws dug into his tunic and he felt them ripping his skin, but he got out from under them, scrambled to his feet, and pressed back against the wall.

Only then he noticed that she wore a collar with a chain which was fastened to a ring in the wall. It stopped her reaching the sty. Keeping his eyes fixed on hers, which were yellow, slanting, and hungry, he began sidling towards the door. Again she growled. 'Now,' he told himself, 'make a dash for it!' He did, and she sprang. He felt her claws in his back, but dived for the doorway and fell over the threshold, out of her reach.

Bleeding, shaken, crestfallen, he ran and walked and ran again until he reached the Viking village. He woke Kol and told him to fetch Isolde to treat his wounds. He wanted her to comfort him too, motherly as she was, but he would never admit as much to his son or any man.

'And don't ask me what happened,' he growled at Kol forbiddingly.

Kol had opened his mouth to do just that, but shut it again before a word had slipped out.

on the brink

Mordec sat on the floor under the window, looking out. The moon had set but the sky was growing lighter. For the first time in his short life he wished it would stay dark forever. His head felt heavy. He pillowed it on an arm which he rested on the stone window-ledge and he felt a breeze stirring his hair, a message that morning was not far off. But at that moment he fell asleep and began to dream.

He dreamt he was walking down a narrow passage towards an enormous pair of double doors. They opened as he approached them and he entered a great hall brightly lit by torchlight. On either side of a long table warriors stood in their armour, facing the door. As he entered they raised their drinking horns and shouted his name. Then a single voice called out 'Welcome to the Hall of the Heroes!' He could see who it was who'd welcomed him: Odin himself, standing at the far end of the table with a raven perched on each shoulder. He knew it was Odin because, although his face was Father Donlock's, he only had one eye. 'Sit down and feast with us,' Odin invited him, and Mordec took an empty chair. He sat, but all the others remained standing. Then Queen Bertha in a mantle of silk, and loaded with ornaments of gold, came and put a book on Mordec's plate. The heroes again lifted their drinking horns, which had miraculously refilled themselves with wine, and shouted, 'Mordec!'

'Mordec! Wake up!' He opened his eyes to find that people were standing about in the room. He was lying on the floor under the window. He felt stiff, and his head ached a little. The lantern had gone out and the grey light of just-before-dawn painted everything and everyone grey. He sat up, rubbed his eyes, felt about for his glasses which had fallen off, and only when they were back on his nose, saw who was there. Four guards, two red feathers and two blue. So it was too late to try and attack them coming in one by one through the door.

A red-feather, perhaps the one who had called his name to wake him up, went on loudly: 'It's time to get ready!'

Mordec got to his feet. Near the door stood Father Donlock with his eyes tightly closed, his hands pressed together with fingertips on chin, and he was murmuring something which Mordec couldn't catch and perhaps wasn't meant to. On the landing, just outside the door, Coo stood with her back to the room, looking to see who was coming up the stairs. She moved aside to let Ally-pally pass. He was bringing Mordec's breakfast basket, and a note from Mel written in curly letters with red ink on the underside of a piece of rabbit skin. Ally-pally held it out to him and mumbled that he'd been told to wait for an answer. Mordec read: 'There will be a crowd at the Bog to see you off, dear boy. Would you consider putting on a tunic I have almost finished running up for you? Vibrant scarlet. It would surely impress itself on the memories of all present. If your answer is yes, tell the bearer and I shall send it over to you at once.'

'Thanks, Ally-pally,' Mordec said. 'Thanks for everything. Please tell the sender of the letter that my answer is no. Definitely no. Thank you.'

Ally-pally patted Mordec on the shoulder and left. He was no sooner gone than a newcomer entered with a springy step; a short, tubby man with a pink smiling face and a jolly manner.

'Morning all!' he greeted the room cheerily. 'It's going to be a lovely day. And hullo there to you, Mordec son of Hauk.' He advanced on Mordec with a hand outstretched. Mordec put out his own hand and the newcomer clasped it warmly. 'Now who do you think I am?' he went on. 'I'll not keep you guessing. I'm your executioner today and my name is Larry. Tell me—have you eaten? If not, we have a few minutes in hand.'

'I don't think I'll eat anything,' Mordec said, 'but I'll have some water.' He pulled the jug out of the basket and drank thirstily.

'What about a bit of a wash,' Larry asked, 'so you'll feel nice and fresh? No? Right then. Let's be on our way.'

A blue-feather guard stepped forward and tied Mordec's wrists together. Father Donlock led the way downstairs. Larry shepherded Mordec before him and the four guards brought up the rear. When they were all assembled outside in front of the tower, a whole platoon of guards marched up. They lined up on either side of Mordec, red feathers on one side, blue on the other. A yellow-feathered captain bawled 'Drummer-boy!', and a very old man began to beat on his drum the slow and muffled beat of a death-march.

'Forwaaard!' the captain commanded, and the procession started off. Father Donlock led the way, followed by the ancient drummer-boy, then the captain, then the two files with Mordec in their midst, and Larry the Executioner last. Mordec felt dazed. 'This cannot be real,' he thought. 'I hope I'm still asleep and only dreaming it.'

Coo closed the tower door with a bang, locked it with the iron key and scurried off towards the castle.

***

Lily, soon followed by Gus, splashed through the shallow waters of the ford a minute or two before the sun came up. A little crowd of castle folk lit the bonfire the moment they saw the horses coming, and cheered as each went by. Though the fire couldn't burn as brightly as it would have done in the dark, the watchers on the ramparts might have seen it had they not all dozed off. As a result of their inattention, no row of flaming torches welcomed Lily to the castle. She pressed her steaming horse straight towards the drawbridge, shouting 'Let us in! Drop the drawbridge! Quick!' But the drawbridge stayed closed, and she had to rein Maelstrom in so suddenly that he reared, and she had to clutch his neck to avoid falling. On the inside, Llewellyn the drawbridge-keeper—a dopey youth known as Porter-Lew, good for nothing but doing tricks with playing cards—struggled to wind it down, but it was firmly stuck, and for the life of him he couldn't discover why.

'Hullo there,' Lily called, her hands cupping her mouth. 'Let us in!'

Porter-Lew heard her, but didn't have the sense to shout back. Fortunately someone else heard her too. Faintly the cries reached the ears of Queen Bertha who had fallen into a light sleep on the windowseat of the Earl's countinghouse. She woke and sat up. 'Lily!' she said, and looked round for the Earl. His snoring told her where he was—fast asleep in his chair. 'Reggie, wake up, they're here!' She shook the old man. 'Come on, take the scroll, ride to the Bog of Brockalee!' And wrapping her cloak about her she hurried to the ramparts to tell Lily he was on his way.

***

In the slowly growing light, Mordec saw dew sparkling on the blades of grass as the execution party marched over it. Larry was right—it was going to be a lovely day.

Soon they were in sight of the bog.

'Halt!' the captain roared. 'Take up your positions.'

The guards formed a semi-circle facing a low platform built of wooden planks which extended over the bog like a small landing-stage. A red-feathered and a blue-feathered guard took hold of Mordec's arms and guided him on to the platform, then took their places in the semi-circle. Father Donlock stood behind them, hands pressed together, head bowed.

Larry the Executioner began to make preparations for the execution, whistling softly to himself, a man happy in his work. From his bag he took out a folded cloth, opened it briskly and spread it on the planks. Next he produced, one by one, six round weighting-stones with leather thongs threaded through them, and set them down on the cloth in a circle, carefully smoothing out their thongs in a radiating pattern. Lastly he pulled out a white cord and laid it neatly in the middle of the circle. The stones with the holes through them reminded Mordec of the small ones which hung along the bottom of his mother's weaving-loom to keep the warp-threads taut and straight, and for a moment his throat tightened, thinking of her.

Larry put a hand on Mordec's shoulder and pointed to the stones. 'My own collection,' he said proudly. 'Nicely matched, as the dough said to the baking pan. Now if you'd like to step this way—stop. Stand right there. Hmm—good posture you've got, boy. Keep your backbone straight in youth and you'll spare yourself a chapter of worry in your old age. Now let me convince you that you can expect nothing less than first-rate service. See the cord? I'm sorry you can't stroke it. If you could, you'd feel how smooth it is. Pure silk. The best. Now come this way.'

He steered Mordec to the bog-end of the wooden platform where he showed him a wooden box-seat

with a low back. 'Look at this now. It's my own tipping device. I thought it up and built it myself,' and
he looked at Mordec with such a smile of pride that
Mordec felt he ought to smile back to show some
appreciation, and he tried rather weakly, but found
himself gulping as he did so.

'It's cunning,' Larry went on. 'Though unfortunately those who benefit from it can't really appreci-
ate it.' He sighed for an imperfect world. 'That's why
I like to demonstrate it beforehand. So let me take
you through the procedure. You are sitting on the
chair. I'm standing behind you like this, the cord goes
round your throat like this—' he mimed, 'and I tie
it like this, and then I do *this*—,' he pulled his fists
sharply apart. 'It's over quicker that way, as the skillet
said to the fried egg. Now the next trick is to know
when it's safe to let it go a little so I can tie a strong
knot, and then—you see this lever?'—he gripped
a stick at the side of the box—I pull it back … like
this …, the seat tips forward like that, and see?—out
of the nest over you go leaving the rest more space
to grow, as the cuckoo said to the thrush's egg.' He
restored the seat to an upright position, and dusted
off his hands.

Mordec felt a wild laughter welling up, but knew
that if he let it out it might make them think he
was crazed with fear. He looked away from Larry's
chair and took a step towards the platform's edge,
drawn by the very thing he dreaded, the dark mud
of the bog.

'Hold him!' Yellow-feather barked.

Larry put his hands on Mordec's shoulders again. 'It's alright, I've got him,' he said. Mordec peered down at the mud and swallowed hard.

At that moment a chorus of untuneful singing reached their ears and Mordec, Larry and Father Donlock turned to see who the singers were. The grey line from Bond House was approaching, led by Bill.

We march towards the rising sun.
Come march with us everyone,
into the age of peace and fun …

Bill brought it to a halt behind the circle of guards. 'Now watch and remember,' he commanded. The heads drooped.

Sticking his thumbs in his belt Bill walked round the guards and on to the platform, smiling his large smile, his eyes sparkling like dew and calling brightly, 'Good-morning!' Mordec expected the guards to stop him, but Yellow-feather said nothing, did nothing. It seemed that the duty-defender had a special right to approach the condemned man. He took Mordec's arm and drew him away from Larry.

'Look,' he whispered, pointing to the horizon. 'The sun's climbing. But it's not too late. You have a few minutes yet to tell me what I want to know and *save yourself.*'

Mordec shook his arm off.

'But *why* won't you tell me where it is?' Bill went on in a hoarse whisper. 'What good can it be to you now?'

'You wouldn't understand,' Mordec said, and turning his back on him, scanned the distance. He was sure that any moment now Jessica would appear.

* * *

'Where is he then, Grandmama?' Lily shouted, and her question was answered as the Earl himself appeared at Bertha's side on the ramparts. Still dressed in his nightclothes, he was clutching a scroll.

'I can't get my chariot out, or my horse,' he called. 'Someone has jammed the winch of the drawbridge.'

'Go out through the kitchen door.' Lily yelled. 'You can ride Roman Ruin.'

'Can't even do that. Someone's barred it from the outside,' the Earl shouted back.

'Look!' Queen Bertha called. She'd just seen Peggy and a dozen kitchen maids and men, every one of them sharper than Porter-Lew, dragging a large open laundry basket towards them. Long, stout rope was tied about it. 'Climb in, Reggie, and down you go!'

They helped the Earl into the basket and slowly—painfully slowly, Lily felt—with a series of drops and jerking stops lowered him to the ground. Gus dismounted and stood ready to help the old man on to Roman Ruin. The Earl clutched and scrambled and slipped until Gus bent his back to make a mounting-block for him.

'You're the new witness for the Defense?' the Earl asked as he settled in the saddle.

'Yes—Mordec wasn't there when we were told about the treaty.'

216

'Enough for a stay of execution,' the Earl said, 'if not for a change of sentence.'

Then he was off, Lily beside him, holding Maelstrom back to keep pace with Roman Ruin but at the same time crying out to the Earl, 'Faster, faster!'

* * *

One by one and two by two, and then in clumps, folk began arriving from nearby Smallbury-on-the-Bog and more distant villages. A muffin-man stood yawning over his tray full of yesterday's unsold muffins. The woman who seemed built out of laundry bundles was there with her baby, never one to miss a public event. Near her stood Dick the shepherd and part-time herald, who had no function at this ceremony and was here as a mere onlooker. Mordec could see no Vikings among them to witness how he would die fighting. And the only person he could fight at this moment was Larry. It would be easy enough to knock him over into the bog, but that would hardly count as a battle to the death.

No. He'd have to rush at the guards and let them cut him down. But if only his hands were free!

'Will you come and take your seat now, please, Mordec son of Hauk,' Larry invited him pleasantly. 'I must tie the stone weights to your limbs. Two on each leg, one on each arm.' But Mordec didn't move.

'Drum!' bawled the captain of the guard, and a drum roll began.

At the same moment the person Mordec had been hoping to see appeared. Leading a party of ladies on ponies, Lady Jessica came riding side-saddle on a palfrey. She and her attendants were all dressed in gauzy white dresses and short white cloaks edged with white feathers. She dismounted and went up to the captain of the guard, who saluted her smartly.

'Will you let me have a last word with the prisoner,' she asked him, 'and hear his messages for his mother and father?'

The captain saluted again by way of consent.

'Drummer-boy,' he yelled, 'hold the drumming!', and at once the withered old 'boy' stopped with his drumsticks in the air.

Jessica went to Mordec. Bill had left the platform and was rearranging the grey line to give it a better view of the condemned boy's last moments. Jessica made her request again, this time to Larry.

'Well, I can't say no, m'lady. There's a minute yet, but barely.' And being the good-natured and considerate fellow he was, he stepped off the platform to give them their minute of private talk.

The guards kept their eyes on Mordec. They watched him take off his glasses and hand them to Jessica. But a sudden roar behind them made them all turn round at once with raised swords. Sir Baz and Omar bore down on them, white horse, white rider. The guardsmen were caught off-balance. They staggered and lunged uselessly as the beast broke through their line. The hooves clomped on the wooden platform. Sir Baz drew his silver sword and Jessica skipped deftly aside and away as the knight leant down and slashed the bonds that bound the prisoner's hands.

'Fight for your life, Mordec!' he cried. 'You and I against the lot of them!'

Mordec's arms were no sooner free than striking out, though Mordec didn't know and would never know whether he was trying merely to protect himself or to aim a blow. Intentionally or not, he hit the first guard who came at him, full on the chest, checking the man's advance and putting him off his stroke with the upraised sword. Mordec stepped to one side and struck the man again from behind, pitching him forward into the bog more by lucky accident than good fighting. Still, his own fists had saved him for a moment and he meant to try again. He got ready for the next man, but no one came. They hesitated to pass Sir Baz, and as they did the knight knocked two of them down. The hind legs of his heavy horse danced on the wooden boards. Mordec stepped backwards to get out of their way and fell into the bog near the mud-coated guardsman, who was clinging to the props of the platform. Mordec too held on, unable to see anything that was happening above. He did not know that Lily and the Earl had just then come galloping up.

Lily reined in Maelstrom on the brink of the bog. The Earl slowed his horse more carefully, but cried out as he did so, *'Hold, in the name of the law!'*

The crowd parted to let him through. On the edge of the wooden platform he stopped and waved his scroll. Everyone looked at him in amazement. The captain of the guard forgot to salute, because of his surprise and because it took him some moments to recognize this old man in scarlet nightgown and nightcap as his master. When he did, he saluted very smartly and barked orders furiously at his men until they were properly and stiffly in line.

It was the young ladies who helped Mordec out of the bog regardless of the damage that the mud did to their white dresses. As he emerged, filthy, and rose to his feet, a cheer went up from the crowd, and even the grey line lifted its heads and smiled stiff smiles. (No one helped the guardsman out until, an hour later, a passing shepherd heard his cries and held out his crook to him.)

'Now see here all present,' the Earl said, raising his voice over the buzz of the crowd and stilling it, 'this document is a Stay of Execution duly signed by me. It says that Mordec son of Hauk must not be executed this morning. A new witness has come forward and there will be another hearing by the court.'

Mordec was too bewildered to take in everything that happened next. He was aware that both Lily and Jessica embraced him, that the Earl shook his hand, that Father Donlock put a hand on his head and muttered something, and that many others came and patted him on the back, including Larry the Executioner who said, 'Not my day after all, but nice for you, lad. And no hard feelings, as the knuckle said to the tombstone.' Neatly then he packed up the tools of his trade and went home to a second breakfast.

For once Bill had nothing to say. He led the grey line away without a snatch of song. The guard was dismissed by the Earl, and the captain marched them off behind the drummer who now struck out a brisker beat. The crowd dispersed, chattering with excitement about the drama that had entertained them so well. 'You should have been there,' folk would say to those who'd missed it, 'it was really well done.'

Mordec was helped up behind Lily on to Maelstrom's back. Jessica trotted up to them on her palfrey, handed Mordec's glasses back to him, and said to Lily, 'To the castle now. I told Peggy to prepare a hot bath for him.'

So she had been perfectly sure, Mordec thought with astonishment, that he would survive and be freed!

discoveries

When the Viking ships came back from Yaremouth, the Earl's court sat again to hear new evidence in the case of Mordec and the bagful of arms. Eric, Gunnar, Little Olaf and Titch all confirmed Gus's testimony that Mordec had not been present when Knefrod had told them about the treaty. Big Hengist asked to see the axe and told the judges that he'd seen it before, on the wall of Knefrod's house—'The house of Kol's dad,' he explained, and the judges gave him their closest attention. He went on to say that while he'd been having a cookery lesson from Isolde in Knefrod's house, he'd seen Kol come in and take the axe from the wall. He was absolutely certain, he said, that this happened on the very day of Mordec's arrest. How could he be so sure, one of the judges asked him. 'Easy,' he said, rocking on his feet and smiling pleasantly as he explained. As all the other boys had sailed south that morning, he and Kol and Mordec had the boys' house to themselves, so of course he'd noticed that Mordec didn't come home to sleep.

'I remember being a bit disappointed. I wanted him to taste my spit-roasted suckling-pig.'

'Didn't you think of going to look for him?' the Earl enquired.

'Naa! Kol told me he'd gone to the castle, and who wouldn't rather sleep in a castle than a cottage?' Big Hengist asked, surprising everyone not just with his memory and powers of observation, but also his insight into human nature. At the same time his words confirmed to the judges that Kol had been behind the plot against Mordec. But why, none of them could fathom. 'Some internal Viking feud,' they concluded, in private conversation among themselves.

* * *

Kol had disappeared with Knefrod before the ships returned. He was more than willing to go wherever his dad might take him, the further the better. He didn't say he was afraid, but he was—of Mordec's revenge, of punishment by his own folk, and even more of Bill and Coo. Bill had warned that he would come for him in the middle of the night in his true dragon shape and scorch and devour him if he so much as mentioned his name.

Kol believed that Knefrod was taking him away to save him, but the truth was that Knefrod was seeking a change of scene for a reason of his own. Sooner or later, he guessed, the story of his visit to Goosegarth would reach his fellow Vikings, and in his head he could hear their laughter, Hakon's guffaw above all.

Isolde told Big Hengist that Knefrod and Kol had gone to London to board a ship for Africa. 'He said he'd kill all the lionesses he could find, and all their cubs.' Big Hengist took this news to Olaf the Shipbuilder, who wondered aloud how he'd break it to Knefrod's wife Gudrun. 'She may be sad,' he said. 'But then again, she may be glad. Who knows?'

Beyond that, no Vikings gave a thought to Knefrod. What was on their minds was gold, and they were impatient to get to the hoard they'd been promised. As soon as Mordec was back in the village, they set off on horseback to meet Lily at the Roman fort. The boys followed on foot with a cartful of spades. Svein the Carter suggested that they get some English labourers to dig for them, but Big Olaf said no, he'd trust nobody with gold but themselves.

They found the young queen waiting for them beside the snakepit, hands on hips, her dark eyes angry.

'If I'd known that Big Hengist could have been a witness for Mordec at his trial, I needn't have promised to give you all this gold just to get Gus to come with me,' she hissed at them through her teeth.

'You should have *asked* Big Hengist,' Harvald said.

'That skunky Bill Hitchem should've,' she snapped, and she spat into the pit as though she wanted to get his name out of her mouth. 'Anyway, I keep my word. So here it is, it's your gold now. You'll find it deep down, under the adders. And I hope they kill you.' She spun round and stamped off, her every movement telling them that she hated them. Gus started after her, but thought better of it and came back.

The Vikings stood round the pit. None looked up or he would have seen Bill Hitchem sitting on the platform where Lily had first told Mordec about the gold. The People's Friend was hugging his head and rocking as if in agony, while saying to himself over and over, 'Adders, not addis. Adders. Adders.'

Mordec peered at the snakes through his glasses, reading on the front of the poisonous heads the tell-tale V of the viper. Hakon threw a spear into the writhing midst of them and gashed one open, but didn't kill it. Bodvar sat on the edge of the hole with his legs dangling, and bent far over trying to reach the bottom with the point of his sword, but it was too short and he nearly lost his balance. He pulled himself back looking pale as if with fear, though he was never afraid of anything.

'Cutting their heads off one by one will take hours,' Svein complained.

'Can you think of a better way?' Harvald asked.

At that moment they heard the sound of wheels and looked up to see the haycart from Goosegarth drawn by the roan and driven by Walter the pigman.

'The old queen sent this,' he said. 'Stuff to get rid of them vipers.'

'What is it?' Big Olaf asked suspiciously, and the Vikings looked at each other with an unspoken question: were the queens trying to trick them after all?

'Can't tell. But Queen B knows a thing or two, that's all I can say,' Walter replied.

They helped him unload three casks.

'Handle it careful now,' Walter said. 'Like this, see.'

He prized off a lid and tipped the barrel carefully, emptying it slowly into the pit. There was a sizzling, smoking, bubbling, and through the evil-smelling fumes the men saw a squirming which was quite different from the sinuous movements they'd watched before. These were death-throes.

'You can pour the rest if you want to,' Walter said. Hakon and Gunnar opened and emptied the other casks and stood back to watch the effect.

Walter took the empty casks back to his wagon. 'She says wait a bit and when it's all seeped away, start digging.'

'Does Queen Lily know Queen Bertha sent us this?' Gus asked.

'Yes,' Walter said, and drove off.

Gus shook his head. 'I don't understand her.'

'She wants us to help her find her mother,' Mordec reminded him.

When the snakes were nothing but a pulpy mess, and the ground had dried under them, men and boys dug with a will that Master Hitchem never inspired in the grey line, although they toiled for others and the Vikings only for themselves.

The gold lay deep. They'd begun to wonder again if they'd been misled and made fools of, when Egil's spade struck wood, and splintered it, so they did not have to lift the huge chest out to see that it contained gold. When they'd heaved it up and taken the broken lid right off, the men plunged their arms into a mass of coins as if they wanted to bathe in them.

'Eyiolf's gold!' Hakon crowed, and the name added an awesome significance to the treasure.

the feast at linkard castle

Sir Cedric had to fight Sir Baz again of course, and a good time was had by all on the castle's own tilting-yard where the grass was now well grown. The decorations for the occasion, by Mel de Gustybuss, were dark blue in compliment to Mordec. Dick the shepherd fulfilled his duties as herald with his usual pitch and precision.

Sir Cedric's violent overthrow—from which, this time, oddly enough, he received hardly any bruises at all—was followed by a feast in the great hall.

Geese were sent from Bertha and Lily's yard; six sheep were brought from the Earl's own meadows; two oxen were contributed by the Vikings, picked from the herd of a landlord under their rule. And that wasn't all. There was soup made by Peggy to Mordec's mother's recipe, and a huge pudding, mixed and steamed by Big Hengist under Isolde's close supervision in the Earl's kitchen. This pudding was stained in patches by the juice of the plums inside it, so Isolde gave it the charming name of Bruised Mordec.

Flutes were played while the goose and meats were eaten, and a trumpet was blown when the pudding was borne in on a silver dish.

Sir Cedric had French wine sent over from his cellars, and the usually sober old judges, the white haired Prosecutor, and even Father Donlock drank more than was good for their reputations. The wine failed to lift Sir Baz's spirits but he talked more than usual, and confided in Mordec that he had gone easy on Sir Cedric because they had become good friends. 'In other circumstances,' Sir Baz said, 'I might have let him win our second bout, but the law being what it is in this earldom, the poor chap has to fight to the death. If he'd got me down, you see, he'd have had no choice. None at all. He'd have had to dispatch me. The privilege of choice belonged only to me. Such is life!'

* * *

A little later Sir Cedric appeared beside Mordec. 'How do you like this … venerable wine?' the knight asked. His speech was hesitant, close to a stammer. He also blinked quite a lot before he said anything. He blinked again now. Too … self-important? Or would you say it deserves its … good opinion of itself?'

Mordec was at a loss for an answer. 'I don't know,' he confessed. 'I'd never tasted wine before I came to England. Nor the water of life.'

'The water of life? For your own dear sake, old man,' Sir Cedric said, and blinked rapidly, 'don't get too … fond of that. Keep off the spirits, stick to … the grape, and you'll live to be … old and healthy. I myself drink nothing but wine. This mellow red comes from my cellars.'

'Don't you live at the castle?'

'Oh no, I have a little villa in the Roman style just outside Smallbury-on-the-Bog. That was where Lady Jessica and Sir Baz … waited for the dawn before sallying forth to … thwart injustice, to … prevent the carrying out of that ill-judged and really quite … inexcusable sentence which had been pronounced on you, old man.'

'Lady Jessica sought my advice,' a voice said on Mordec's other side. It was Mel come to join them, now dressed in dark green. 'For the scene of the rescue, I mean. And I said, "White, m'lady, the gauziest white". I explained that she and her ladies must appear to be the most delicate and helpless of creatures to keep the guard from suspecting anything. "As harmless, as weak, as girlish, as inactive," I said, "as is humanly possible." And you supported me in that, didn't you, Sir Cedric?'

'Entirely. Totally. I believed it was … a wise ploy, and so it proved. And jolly lucky it was that they … waited with me, considering that they'd never have got out of the castle. Strange … business, that winch getting stuck like that. I must tell you frankly, I suspect foul play.'

'I'm sure of it,' Mel said. He turned again to Mordec. 'How do you like the colours I've chosen for the ladies this evening? Pheasant shades, I call them. Mostly this deepest, richest green. Look, the Earl himself agreed to wear a green cloak. I made Lady Jessica's gown with my own hands. I've been long guarding that burgundy red in the hope that she'd accept it eventually. And doesn't she look well in it? It makes her cheeks glow.'

'I think that's because of *my* burgundy rather than … yours,' Sir Cedric said, blinking, and they both looked fondly at Jessica, and raising their goblets to each other and Mordec they toasted 'our Lady Jessica and all the lovely ladies of the court'.

Mordec drank thirstily, and when he put down his goblet he said, 'Not even the Romans feasted better than this. I've read about a Roman feast.'

'Have you really? Bless my soul, an intellectual Viking! My dear chap, you are … a walking Contradiction in Terms.'

Before Mordec could ask him to explain what he meant, Bill Hitchem appeared. He stood on the other side of the table in his usual red and green, smiling and bowing. Having recovered from the double disappointment of neither getting the gold nor seeing Mordec executed, he'd decided to make the best of things as they stood. 'Nice to have you with us,' he said. 'I'm glad I was able to play my part. I knew all along that our case was good. No need to thank,' he said and strutted off, waving away the gratitude that was ever his due.

'I'm going to ask the Earl,' Sir Cedric said, blinking, 'to let me practice mortal … combat on that fellow. I'm getting a little rusty for want of … villains in these times. In my estimation, that chappie … qualifies. D'you agree?'

'Oh, come come,' Mel said, 'He used to be a lot worse, you must admit. I made the man almost human.'

'Well, should I fail to impale him on my … lance at the first attack,' Sir Cedric said, 'you may have him back again … to complete the transformation.'

'Agreed,' Mel said, and the three goblets were raised again.

The Vikings, men and boys, were seated together at one table, except Big Olaf, Harvald and Hakon, who'd been placed in seats of honor beside or near Queen Bertha. They were doing their best to entertain that regal lady with stories of conquest which seemed neither to please nor displease her. They thought her very mysterious. She had brought the little lioness on a short chain which was now fastened to a ring in the stone floor. The beast sat beside Queen Bertha's chair, upright, very still, occasionally licking her black lips or blinking her yellow eyes. Hakon could hardly take his own eyes off the animal. On an impulse he reached for a large slab of red oxmeat, pushed it under his tunic to press against his chest, and when it was warm and salty he pulled it out and flung it down before the lioness. She swallowed it and wiped her face with her big pink tongue a number of times, luxuriously. Queen Bertha waited for Hakon's loud laughter to quieten, then she told him, softly, huskily, 'I knew a Viking once who fed her like that. She liked the flavor of the man on the meat. So one day she ate him.' Hakon's laughter stopped abruptly and the smile died on his face.

The long trumpet sounded. Sir Baz bowed to the Earl and turned to a group of pages, ladies and gentlemen including the captain of the guard, and the clerks of the law court who'd assembled on one side of the hall, dressed in Mel's 'pheasant colours'. Sir Baz raised his arms to conduct his own composition. A page sang the solo parts, the rest the chorus:

*Mordec the Viking from the land of ice and snow
came to conquer England with a sword*

Chorus: with a sword

*He was captured and condemned, by his just but
    ruthless foe,
to be strangled till he croaked, with a cord*

Chorus: with a cord

*Friendless and alone like a villain he must go
to be choked on the edge of a bog*

Chorus: of a bog

*where vipers dare not creep or willows even weep
but a man may be drowned like a dog*

Chorus: like a dog

*Mordec did not shrink when they shoved him in the
    drink but like all the famous heroes of his land*

Chorus: of his land

*he fought, and he bought his life with his blood
felling fifty-seven guardsmen with one hand*

Chorus: with one hand.

Everyone applauded, and they all looked at Mordec as they clapped and cheered. Mordec suddenly had to take his glasses off and pay close attention to the business of polishing them thoroughly with a comer of his cloak.

'Now,' said the Earl, and the hall fell silent. 'Mordec son of Hauk. You are honest and brave. I am sorry you were put through such an ordeal in my country. I hope you will think of us as friends despite what happened.'

'Why,' Mordec said, a little hesitantly, 'you're the best friends anyone could have. And that song, well, it's a very good song. I mean to say, thank you for it. But I must also say that it isn't entirely true, of course. I only knocked down one guardsman. And I wasn't friendless—I had more friends than I knew. And I didn't really bleed, and … The truth is,' he went on in a more spirited manner, 'that I'm not really the hero of the story. Lily is. Queen Lily. We should sing about her. And Queen Bertha. And Sir Baz. And Lady Jessica, and Sir Cedric, and the Earl, and Peggy, and Ally-pally, and Walter, and Gus, and Big Hengist. I owe them all more than gold could repay. And then there were the folk who stayed up all night to light the bonfire and—more people than I even know the names of. I'll never forget. I give you my word that I'll never forget. And—and you did all this for a Viking, although we burnt your libraries. And—'

They waited for him to go on, but he didn't know what else to say, what words would do for what he owed his friends, if he could find them in the mist that was filling his head. He was saved from having to say anything more by Father Donlock, who stepped out where all could see him and said. 'Mordec son of Hauk surprises me. Not with his strength and courage. We expect no less of a Viking. But with his lack of vanity and boastfulness. With his modesty and humility. Now, Sir Baz, true or not true, your song has a rousing ring to it, so let's have it again.'

Mordec looked round the hall for Lily. She'd been sitting close to him for a time and had shown him a sword. 'It was Knefrod's,' she'd whispered, 'but it's mine now.' She hadn't said how she'd captured it.

She went out while Mordec was making his speech. In the servants' hall, where men and maids were downing ale and goose and pudding, she found Porter-Lew doing his card tricks, and asked him if he'd found out why the drawbridge winch had got stuck. Yes, he said, it'd had an iron bar jammed in it, and Mistress Pillikin was the one who'd done it. 'I asked her, "Now why'd you go and do a thing like that?" And she said, "To strike a blow for the underdog." And I said, "What underdog?" And she said, "Me, to start with".'

There were a lot of left-overs from the feast, as Lady Jessica had expected there would be. She sent orders to the chief cook and the captain of the guard that all the good food left over was to be sent tomorrow under armed guard to Bond House for the men and boys in grey, and that the guards were to wait there until the bondsmen had eaten their fill. She gave no reason for this last part of the order, but everybody knew that it was in case Bill and Coo came along to share it by taking it all away. And Queen Bertha promised to send a pig to the guards, to make up for the injuries Sir Baz had inflicted on their pride.

Among the last of the merrymakers to go to bed on that memorable night were Dick the Shepherd and Larry the Executioner. An eager crowd of listeners gathered round Dick in the main yard of the castle— servants, gardeners, grooms, the smith, the tanner, the saddler, the fletcher, the falconer, weavers, seam- stresses and such—to hear his eye-witness account of the Viking's rescue. Three times Dick repeated his tale, each time recalling more thrilling details. At the last telling, Mordec was already in the chair and the cord touching his throat when—

'Ho and below! The white knight rode up and snatched him from the brink of annie-o-lashun.'

At this the ancient drummer boy, wanting to re- mind everyone that he'd attended the occasion in an official capacity, shrilled out: 'It weren't that close, were it? Not really, Master Executioner?'

But Larry was not a man to spoil other men's yarns. 'It was very close,' he said, nodding and smiling. 'They turned up to save the boy in the last few sec- onds of the last minute. Cutting it fine, as December said to the wind.'

summer's end

Mordec visited Sir Cedric in his 'little villa' and found it was a big pink house built round a courtyard in which they sat and drank wine. Sir Cedric told him how wine was made in France, and he had a flask opened and its pale gold contents poured for them by a Scot in an apron. 'My cellarman,' Sir Cedric said. Blinking rapidly. 'Deaf-mute. Ideal … servant.' He showed Mordec the cellars and stables. And lent him a good-natured grey filly named Blanche.

Mordec went riding with Gus and Lily, and learnt to ride well enough. But neither he nor Gus could hold on to a galloping mount with their knees only, while aiming and shooting arrows as Lily could.

Mordec had a question for Lily. One day as they were riding side by side and Gus was some way ahead, he said to her, 'You didn't have to promise them the gold. They would have told the truth in the Earl's court anyway. We Vikings have laws and trials and judgments. Why didn't you and your grandmother spend the gold? You could have rebuilt your palace—or paid quite a lot of soldiers with all that.'

'We didn't use it because we always expected Eyiolf to come back for it and then we would ask him for my mother in return for telling him where we buried his gold. Now I've given Viking gold back to you Vikings, I want friendly help to find my mother. She's the real ruler of the Fenreach. She's the one who could make the other English rulers unite to get our land back. The whole of Northumbria now has been taken over by Northmen.'

'Have you asked any of our men if they'll help you find your mother?'

'No. But now I'm asking you.'

'Me? Why me?'

'You can read. You can speak. Eyiolf's men will need to be properly *asked*. It's no use sending warriors to fight them. He was the biggest strongest cruelest warrior of you all. But you—well, you're a Viking, but also a—a person, if you understand what I mean.'

'You praise me, but I … Tell me what it is you want me to do? What you think I *can* do?'

'You can find out where Eyiolf's men are and then come with me to ask them to let her go. Will you do that? Remember, you're in debt to me, Mordec son of Hauk!'

'Yes. I am. And I will do what you ask. You must find a way to let me know when you are ready. And yes, I will find out where Eyiolf's men are.'

Lily, Mordec, Gus and Horsa went with the Earl's pack to hunt a boar. It tossed four dogs before it was killed. Horsa dipped his sword-tip and spear-head in its blood. 'They're thirsty,' he explained to Mordec.

Little Hengist's curiosity was aroused by Mordec's description of the lever system which worked the execution chair, and he went to examine it. He found the inventor himself at the bogside, oiling the works. Larry was delighted to give an interested visitor a demonstration, and encouraged him to pull the lever himself. Little Hengist's considered opinion was that the device was 'neat, but might work better with a coil-spring'.

Larry wasn't sure about that but said he'd construct a model to test the idea.

Little Hengist asked to work on it with him, and went every day to potter about with the good-natured executioner in his shed near the castle.

As the day drew near for the Vikings' voyage home, the hundred men who'd sailed south on the first morning returned in cheerful mood, their ships freighted with grains, and bronze ornaments, silk, linen, woollen clorh, dyes and ironware, for which they'd bartered. A few hours later the forty-two who'd ridden west turned up in grumpy mood. Mordec asked Harvald the Armourer what they'd brought back and Harvald said, 'Experience.'

On the last day, cartsful of tin were trundled from the earldom to the landing-stage and loaded directly into the ships.

Sir Cedric's deaf-mute Scot came to fetch Blanch the filly. He handed Mordec a flask of wine, a parting gift from his master, and to Mordec's surprise murmured in his ear, 'Och, the wine's gud for tanning the innards of a mon. The water o'life's the gud stuff. But wist—nae word did I say t'ye.'

In the last hour, when all else was stowed, the gold was brought out of a hiding-place known only to Olaf and

Harvald and four others. It had been packed into an oaken chest fastened with iron locks and chains. As the six men heaved it into Big Olaf's ship the rest cheered. Then Hakon, in armour and holding his sword, sat on it.

Women and girls crowded on to the landing-stage. Some of them shed tears. Isolde wept noisily as she hugged Big Hengist and handed him a large basket full of good things to eat.

'I'm not roping your ship unless I have to,' Big Olaf told Mordec. 'You can show us what you've learnt about sailing.'

Mel arrived dressed in sad brown and mounted on a tawny donkey. He was the bearer of a present for Mordec from Lady Jessica. Father Donlock, he said, had chosen it, but he himself had wrapped it in yellow silk. He put the packet in Mordec's hand, murmured 'Dear boy,' and rode off again, head bowed, wiping his eyes. Mordec unwound the silk and found a small book bound in red leather, its title stamped in gold: *A Bestiary*.

When everyone else had gone to the ships, Mordec and Gus still lingered in front of their house. Mordec was turning the pages of his book, while Gus seemed to be waiting for something. Hearing the sound of hooves, he looked up expectantly, and moments later Lily came trotting along on her stallion. She jumped down, ran to Mordec and seized his hands. 'Next year,' she said, 'you'll help me find my mother.'

'Yes,' Gus said, 'and I'll …'

But she didn't seem to want to hear what Gus would do. She remounted and was turning Maelstrom away before he'd called 'Lily!' again. He called her name twice more, but she gave no answer, nor even glanced back at him. His disappointment was plain to see.

Mordec put a hand on his shoulder. 'Come on, Gus,' he said, 'we need you to captain the ship.'

Smoothly the ships moved on wings of dipping oars down the River Nijn towards the sea, Foal of the Foam last in line. On the edge of the furthest watery meadow on which man or beast could find a foothold, Sir Baz waited on his white charger. He raised his sword high in salute and the sun struck arrows of light from it. When Mordec saw the lone knight he stood up and raised his arms. His glasses caught the sunshafts and flashed them back. Their message was:

Farewell